1

AMSTERDAM - 23 SEPTEMBER 2023

THURSDAY 07.01 AM

As customers approached the cafe, the alluring white interior caught their eyes. It was even more intriguing up close, beckoning them to step inside and discover all the wonders it held.

The newly opened place is already drawing much attention, with many people streaming in to check it out. It's impressive to see such a level of interest so soon after the opening, and it's clear that people are eager to explore everything the place has to offer.

Jade, a young girl with tousled brown hair, sits perched on a cushioned window seat overlooking the busy city street below. The streetlights streamed through the tall window, casting a soft glow on her face as she sipped her usual oat milk cappuccino. She watches intently as a sea of people rush to their respective jobs, each lost in their thoughts and agendas. Despite the chaos outside, she focuses entirely on handcrafting a new song.

The coffee shop is known as "Blond Amsterdam Store & Cafe." It offers a stunning view of the street outside, making it a perfect spot for coffee lovers who want to enjoy their favourite beverage and the views.

The bustling street was adorned with numerous bicycles, parked haphazardly along the sidewalk and weaving through the traffic flow.

Jade's pulse quickens with anticipation as she slowly lifts the sleek lid of her laptop, revealing the vividly illuminated screen that glows in the dim light of the cafe's room. She can't help but feel a sense of excitement bubbling up inside of her as she runs her fingers over the smooth skin, eager to explore the endless possibilities that await her.

With a deep breath, she dons her noise-cancelling headphones, enveloping herself in a cocoon of serene silence. As she gazes at the screen, her mind brims with ideas and inspiration, ready to plunge into a world of boundless creativity and unparalleled productivity.

Jade is now searching for the perfect song on her phone.

As soon as she opens the song writing application, she begins the process of writing and deleting various words in a seemingly random fashion.

Jade's story begins in Guatemala, where she was born and spent the first few years of her life. However, due to her father's job, her family moved around Europe quite a bit during her childhood. She spent a few years in Germany with her father before settling in London to pursue her dream of becoming a songwriter.

Jade's passion for music was evident from a young age, and she dedicated herself to honing her skills as a songwriter. After a couple of years in London, she packed up and moved to Amsterdam, a city she had long dreamed of living in. The vibrant music scene and the city's artistic culture called to her, and she knew it was the perfect place to continue her musical journey. Today, Jade continues to live and create in Amsterdam, drawing inspiration from the city's rich history and diverse community.

Amidst the hustle and bustle of people rushing to their daily routines, Jade's attention has shifted to the weather outside the coffee shop. She notices the gentle rustling of leaves as the wind blows through the trees and the faint sound of distant thunder that echoes in the background. The sky is a mix of dark grey and soft blue, with heavy clouds that promise rain. Despite the urgency of her *morning tasks, Jade pauses for a moment to take in the beauty of the natural world around her.*

The city slowly moves towards autumn as the grey clouds overtake the sky. It's as if the weather sets the perfect mood to snuggle up with a warm blanket and a cup of hot cocoa.

Looking up at the sky, she sees the clouds forming an enormous shape, with their fluffy, white and grey formations interweaving to create a breath-taking sight.

There's a high likelihood of rain pouring down any moment now.

Jade appears preoccupied with something, lost in her thoughts and with a faraway look. Her mind is racing, possibly with many different ideas or concerns.

As time ticks by, Jade becomes increasingly preoccupied with her task. She sits at her usual seat, her fingers dancing across the keyboard as she types a few words, then backspaces to delete them. Her eyes dart back and forth between the screen and the window as if searching for inspiration from the world beyond her computer. Despite her efforts, the words seem to elude her grasp, slipping away as quickly as she can type them.

As she glances to her right, she notices a man sitting in the adjacent seat. He has a relaxed posture, with his left hand holding onto a laptop and his right hand grasping a coffee cup. A gentle smile graces his face as he appears lost in thought.

As she catches the guy's eye, a playful smile spreads across her face, drawing him in with an irresistible innocence.

The coffee shop is becoming more crowded as people come and go, but suddenly the street becomes empty.

As Jade watches the leaves gently fluttering down from the trees, she feels like she's witnessing a magical moment that's just for her. Then suddenly, her attention was captured by a strikingly handsome guy strolling by with his bicycle in tow.

She keeps looking up as her favourite song plays on her phone.

With a focused and unwavering look, Jade fixates her eyes on the guy, delving deep into his soul with a piercing gaze.

As the guy feels someone's eyes on him, he turns around with his headphones dangling around his neck, exuding a charm that's hard to resist.

As the two individuals look at each other, their eyes meet silently. Time seems to stand still as they gaze fixed on each other; the tension is palpable in the air. After several seconds of intense staring contest, the guy loses focus and accidentally collides with someone with his bicycle. He had been so distracted by the captivating presence of Jade that he ignored his surroundings.

Jade's smile is like a ray of sunshine on a cloudy day; it's the kind that can brighten up people's entire mood. Her smile is contagious, and he can't help but feel happy when he sees it. It's a genuine expression of joy; he knows she's thrilled at that *moment. It's a beautiful thing to witness, and it makes him appreciate the little moments of happiness in life, that little moment. So, the guy, feeling a bit embarrassed, smiles in response.*

2

AMSTERDAM - 24 NOVEMBER 2023

Simone and Jade are curled up on the comfortable beige sofa, which is covered with a soft throw and surrounded by fluffy cushions. The TV is on low volume, and a nature documentary is playing, showcasing the beauty of the African Savannah. However, Simone and Jade are engrossed in their world, engaging in a deep conversation with occasional laughter and animated gestures. Their eyes sparkle with excitement, and their faces glow with joy as they share their thoughts and feelings. The warm, cosy ambience of the room and the soothing sound of the narrator's voice create a serene atmosphere, adding to the peacefulness of the moment.

"I can give it a shot with you. I've been interested in trying it out myself." Simone says, smiling.

"It's amazing that in just two months, I've managed to transform the way you think about it completely." Says Jade, smiling at Simone.

"Are you sure about your decision to adopt a vegan lifestyle? It can be pretty challenging." Jade asked.

"Can you imagine how hard it was to walk up to you that day in September? But here we are now. I think transitioning to a vegan lifestyle could be less challenging."

Jade and Simone can't help but burst into laughter as Simone jokingly shoves Jade onto the soft, plush sofa and playfully begins to tickle her. Their infectious laughter fills the room as Simone's fingers dance along Jade's sides.

Jade can't stop laughing. "Can you stop? I hate it."

"I know you do!"

He leaned in and pressed his lips softly against her cheek, then slowly moved to her lips, savouring the moment.

"Do you know what I've been thinking? How much do you love me?" Simone asks.

Jade opens her arms as wide as she can.

"Is it enough?"

"Do you think it's enough?" Simone asks.

Jade smiles. "No!".

As they stand close, gazing into each other's eyes, he leans in slowly, his breath warm against her cheek. Her heart races as she anticipates his kiss, and when his lips finally meet hers, she responds eagerly, feeling every sensation as their mouths move together in a passionate dance. The taste of his lips, the touch of his hand on her back, and their breathing are etched into her memory as she loses herself in the moment.

Their apartment is a lovely and intimate space that exudes comfort and warmth. Despite its small size, it's thoughtfully designed with clever storage solutions and cosy furnishings, making it spacious and inviting. The soft lighting and warm colour palette add to the ambience, creating a relaxing and cosy atmosphere that makes it the perfect place to unwind after a long day.

Simone and Jade share a profound love for each other, a bond built on mutual respect, understanding, and passion for life.

"Okay, I think I'm going to have an early night," Simone stands up from the sofa. "Tomorrow, I must wake up early for an important audition."

"Oh yes, I'll come to bed later; I will finish watching this show, and I promise I'll join you as soon as it's over."

Simone begins to undress as he walks towards the bedroom, casting a sultry gaze towards Jade. With a mischievous grin, he invites her to join him in bed, beckoning her with a playful wink.

"Good night, babe. Sleep well," says Jade.

She knew exactly what he had in mind but ignored his advances and kept watching the TV. Simone smiles at Jade.

"Good night, love."

AMSTERDAM - 25 NOVEMBER 2023, the morning after.

Simone is a 29-year-old aspiring theatre actor. He's about to face his biggest audition yet. With his heart pounding and nerves on edge, he's determined to give it his all and make his dreams a reality.

He's been awake since 4 am, desperately trying to squeeze in more study time for that upcoming casting. That's the situation Simone finds himself in. But hoping all that hard work will surely pay off in the end.

Jade's morning routine starts with her trusty phone alarm ringing at dawn - 6 AM sharp.

She can hear raindrops hitting the ground outside as she lay in bed. The heavy drops make a thudding sound as they hit the pavement. The pitter-patter of the rain creates a soothing ambience, and she can almost feel the freshness that it brings. The sound of the rain is powerful yet calming and fills the room with a sense of tranquillity that is hard to describe. Overall, it's a beautiful experience that she likes to be in.

Simone enters the bedroom upon hearing the alarm going off.

"Good morning, Amore. Do you want a cup of coffee? It's still hot."

The streetlights seep through the window as Jade slowly begins to stretch her arms and legs while still lying in bed.

"Would you please bring it to me? I'd like to have it in bed." Jade answered.

As Simone strolls back into the kitchen, the aroma of freshly brewed coffee hits his senses. His eyes land on a colourful array of mugs displayed on the shelf. Without hesitation, he grabs one that immediately catches his attention. The ceramic mug features a black background with the words "hate is heavy, let it go" written in bold white font. The phrase is a gentle reminder to release negative feelings and focus on positivity.

As he enters the room, carrying a hot cup of coffee, he carefully pours a generous amount of creamy oat milk, creating a swirl of steam and aroma filling the air.

The mug has a sturdy handle for a comfortable grip and a smooth finish for an enjoyable drinking experience.

Simone places the mug on the nightstand and kisses Jade's forehead.

"How do you feel?"

"I'm feeling great!" Jade says. "Can you remind me what time your audition is scheduled for?"

"Is there something special that you're planning?"

The corners of Jade's lips turned up, revealing a joyous expression.

"Probably."

"My audition is at 8:00 AM. Then, I will meet Lucian for a catch-up, and then I'll be free."

Jade's slender fingers carefully wrap around the warm ceramic mug, lifting it off the nightstand and bringing it closer to her body as she sits down on *the edge of the bed. She takes a deep breath, inhaling the soothing aroma of the steaming beverage before taking a sip.*

She feels the heat from the cup. "Uh, that's hot! How long has it been?"

" Do you mean with Lucian? We haven't met in ages. We both have been swamped."

Jade starts sipping her coffee.

"Would you like to come with me to visit one of Amsterdam's largest libraries?" *Jade asks.*

"Probably," *Simone answers.*

"I can come home around 10 A.m. Right now, I'm just thinking of the audition, and I'm excited to give it my all!"

"I believe in you and your ability to nail that audition! I'm confident that you will perform exceptionally and impress the judges with your natural talent. "

"Thank you, babe!"

Simone walks briskly back to the kitchen, a determined look on his face, and reaches for his bag, which he had left on the counter, making sure to pack all the necessary items before heading out. Jade looks up as he walks back into the room, a smile spreading across her face. He leans in to kiss her, his touch sending shivers down her spine. With a final goodbye, he grabs his bag and keys from the table and walks out the door.

Simone hopped on his bicycle and sped into traffic on a dark, cold day.

The torrential downpour drenching the city has finally stopped, leaving behind a refreshed and glistening landscape.

Simone was born in Italy and always had a deep-seated curiosity about the world beyond his hometown. After completing his studies, he embarked on a journey across Europe, eager to explore different cultures and absorb new experiences. Simone's travels took him to various countries with unique customs and traditions, which he eagerly embraced.

As he travelled, Simone discovered a new passion - acting in theatre. He was drawn to how theatre allowed him to express himself creatively, and he felt at home on stage, performing in front of an audience. Simone was not content to let his dream remain a mere fantasy. Instead, he dedicated himself to learning everything he could about acting, from the art of improvisation to the subtleties of character development.

He hopped on his bike and peddled to one of his all-time favourite coffee spots to grab his second cup of the day.

The traffic can be pretty heavy during rush hour, especially on major highways and in urban areas. It can cause delays and frustration for commuters trying to reach their destinations on time. However, traffic can also be lighter when riding a bicycle, making for him a more pleasant driving experience.

The name of the coffee shop on the top of the building is "Blond Amsterdam Store & Cafe."

Simone walks through the door of the cosy cafe, greeted by the aroma of freshly brewed coffee and the soft hum of chatter from the patrons seated at small tables. He takes a moment to scan the room, taking in the warm lighting and rustic decor before going to the counter to place his order.

"Good morning; how are you today?"

The barista turned to Simone when he heard his voice.

"How are you feeling, Simone? I'm doing well; I'm always busy here."

Due to his frequent visits, Simone has become a familiar face at the coffee shop.

"Today, I am feeling confident and excited about my upcoming audition. I have put in a lot of effort to prepare for it, and I hope my hard work will pay off and result in a fantastic performance."

The barista standing at the counter of the coffee shop begins to prepare Simone's oat latte, anticipating Simone's request and taking care to grind the coffee beans to the perfect consistency. As he waits for the espresso to finish brewing, he turns to the barista warmly, appreciating the skilful artistry that goes into every cup of coffee.

"What is the casting for?"

" Have you ever heard of the Boom Chicago show? It's a comedy play."

"Yeah, it's viral."

"It's a big gig, yes."

Simone eagerly reaches out to grab the steaming oat latte from the friendly barista's hand, feeling the cup's warmth and the comforting aroma of the coffee filling his senses.

" Enjoy your latte, And good luck with your audition! I'm sure you'll get it."

"Thank you"

The intern working at the cafe shop is a significant factor in attracting many customers.

Simone sits at his usual table and eagerly opens the pages of "The Hidden Life of Trees," a book he had been eyeing for weeks. As he flips through the pages, he takes in the earthy scent of the old tome and runs his fingers across the smooth, yellowed pages. The chatter and clinking of dishes around him become background noise as he delves into the fascinating world of trees.

The rich aroma of freshly brewed coffee fills the room as he takes a moment to savour the first sip. With each turn of the page, he becomes fully immersed in the world of an exciting new book, losing track of time and his surroundings. As the minutes tick by, he finds himself lost in the story, savouring every sip and every word.

Simone's facial expression transformed into calm and ease, not even worrying about what the audition would be like.

The cafe is buzzing with customers, bringing their energy and excitement to the space making it a lively and vibrant spot.

Simone reaches for his pocket and pulls out his favourite pair of earphones. He gently places them into his ears and adjusts them for maximum comfort. As the music starts playing, he returns to reading and getting lost in the melodic tunes.

3

As Jade strolls down the hallway, she can't help but feel a sense of excitement as she approaches the kitchen, eager to bring order to the chaos.

Her face lights up with a joyous smile when a spotless and well-organised space greets her. It's no secret that she adores a pristine and tidy environment.

The kitchen's interior is where Jade and Simone's culinary magic occurs. Its where delicious aromas fill the air and meals are prepared with care and attention to detail.

If there's one thing Jade loves doing, it's scouring the internet for the latest and most delicious recipes! The kitchen walls surrounding Jade are adorned with colourful tiles and sleek granite countertops. The cabinets are neatly arranged, and the appliances are modern and efficient. Every inch of their kitchen's interior is designed to maximise functionality while creating a warm and inviting atmosphere.

Jade heats a pan and pours oat milk to make pancakes.

She starts cutting strawberries, berries, and bananas and placing them on a plate.

She is currently experiencing a high level of contentment and joy. She sipped her now-warm coffee while dancing and whistling her favourite song.

As she savours the delicious pancakes, she pulls out her phone and begins to browse through the photos, seated comfortably at the kitchen table.

As she scrolls through the phone's photo gallery, she comes across snapshots of herself and Simone relishing in the tourist attractions of Paris and Milan. The camera captures their joyous expressions as they visit iconic landmarks and indulge in the local cuisine. The picturesque scenery and vibrant atmosphere of both cities are beautifully captured in the photos, making her feel like she is still a part of that exciting journey.

Her heart flutters as she gazes at her phone, feeling pure bliss in these fleeting moments.

Suddenly, Jade's phone buzzes: it's a Zoom call from her mom.

"Hey!"

"Hey mom, you, okay?"

"I'm afraid I have some bad news to share with you."

Through the phone, Maria, Jade's mum, sits on a sofa by the window in her living room during the video call.

"What happened, Mom?"

"I am sorry...Cutie has passed away."

Maria sat with her head in her hands, tears cascading down her face. The image of the dog she had been thinking about consumed her, filling her with a deep sadness that she couldn't contain. Her heart felt heavy and burdened.

"What? How did that happen? How did it come to be? He was okay the last time I spoke to you. When was it? Two days ago?"

"Yeah, but remember when we got him at 9, despite what they said about his age? I knew he was old but didn't expect it to happen anytime soon."

Although she hasn't had many opportunities to spend time with Cutie, Jade cherishes his presence.

As she sits there, she catches sight of a picture frame perched on a nearby table. With a timid smile, she reaches out to grasp it - a cherished memory of Cutie and her mom, frozen in time. She recognises that Cutie holds a special place in her mother's heart and has been a constant source of comfort and companionship for her.

"I'm sorry to hear that... what will we do now?"

It's hard not to notice the growing sadness etched onto Jade's mother's face.

"Is now the right time to get another dog? Because I'm worried, I'll miss him too much."

"What do you think?" Jade asked.

The moment the question was asked, Maria's face lit up with excitement and anticipation. "Have you ever scrolled through a page of dogs up for adoption? It's impossible not to fall in love with every one of them. I recently did just that, and let me tell you, my heartstrings were tugged by so many adorable pups looking for their forever home."

"Well, you could adopt one of them then. That sounds wonderful, mom! You won't be alone but must get a younger one this time."

As Jade looks up at her mom, a sweet smile spreads across her face, filling the room with warmth and happiness.

"Okay, I'll think about it," Maria exclaimed. "I am going to sleep now. It's almost midnight here, and I apologise for the bad news."

As she gazes at her mother, she again reaches for her coffee cup. She takes a sip to her lips, only to reveal that the once warm and inviting liquid has become a cold and unappetising concoction. "Ugh, cold coffee," she remarks with a hint of disgust. Her face takes a weird, strange shape.

"No, it's okay. Thank you for calling me Mum. I love you."

"I love you too."

Jade finishes the video call, feeling a warm glow in her heart. She sets her phone down on the table, smiling as she takes a moment to bask in the afterglow of the conversation.

As she rises to her feet, she gracefully picks up the cup and walks towards the sink to dispose of the stale, lukewarm coffee.

She walks over to the table to clear her space. She takes a deep breath, stretches her arms and gets to work. With each quick movement, she feels satisfied as the table becomes more organised.

4

Simone is focused on reaching his audition on time as he peddles his bike. The street is alive with movement, with cars honking and bicycles weaving through the traffic. The bustling street is becoming even more crowded as Simone makes his way closer to the audition location, quickly navigating through the hustle and bustle.

Dark clouds have gathered in the sky, and water droplets are falling from them, gently tapping against the street's pavement. The familiar sound of rain has returned once again. When he reaches the designated location, he carefully parks his bicycle, ensuring it is securely fastened with a sturdy lock to prevent theft or damage. After ensuring his bike is safe, he enters the building, taking note of his surroundings and any potential hazards along the way.

The nervous anticipation for the upcoming audition process has resurfaced. As he stepped into the building, his eyes were greeted with a spacious yet cosy interior that exuded a professional ambience. The entrance room was tastefully decorated with warm lighting, plush chairs, and a sleek table at the centre. The walls were adorned with posters of famous actors and actresses, adding to the air of excitement.

As he scans his surroundings, he notices a complete absence of any movement or audible sounds, leaving him with an eerie feeling of stillness and desolation.

Simone, with anticipation and excitement, walks towards the audition room. As he enters the room, he's met with an eerie silence and a cold breeze that sends shivers down his spine. He looks around and realises that the room is empty. The chairs, *tables, and equipment are all in their respective places, yet there is no sign of anyone.*

Simone's heart races as he pulls out his phone to check the audition time. His eyes scan the screen, and his heart sinks as he sees that the audition call was scheduled for 7 A.M. He had missed his opportunity to showcase his talent. His mind races with questions as he tries to understand how he could have made such a grave error.

"Fuck it..." Simone exclaimed.

Simone cautiously peeks through the door, scanning the area for any signs of movement or presence.

He turns quickly to his right towards the info point.

With each step, he moves closer to the other entrance, his eyes scanning the crowd for any sign of the person he's trying to find.

Walking towards the reception, he immediately notices the warm and inviting atmosphere. The space is bright and well-lit, with large windows letting in natural light. The walls are painted in a calming shade of cream, and comfortable chairs are arranged in a cosy seating area. The reception desk is sleek and modern, with a friendly receptionist ready to assist anyone. Overall, the reception room feels welcoming and professional.

Simone's steps quickened as he showed signs of nervousness.

"Hey... hi, I read the timesheet wrong. Is there anyone around here whom I can talk to?"

"Everyone has left already... they waited more than 20 minutes for you to arrive."

"Oh wow... Do you have the casting director's number? I can maybe give him a call..."

Simone meets the Receptionist's gaze, sensing a shift in the air. He was hoping for a warm and welcoming reception, but instead, he could feel a palpable tension in the air around the Receptionist.

"Sorry, but unfortunately, that's not an option; I can't just give his personal details to the first actor who walks in."

"Okay, is there anything I can do to book it again or anything like that? I have an impeccable record of punctuality. But today, I don't know what happened. I woke up very early so I could take my time to relax before this audition…"

Simone's countenance becomes even more subdued as he realises, he has to convince the receptionist to change their stance.

"Unfortunately, I just realised that I had misread the time. This experience has reinforced my commitment to punctuality, and I believe it's a trait that can benefit everyone if I have to be honest." Tries to explain Simone.

"I'm sorry, I can't help you now. You also know how it works. No second chances."

"Only in this stupid world," Simone commented.

Simone looks around, seeking somebody else's help.

Simone is now getting impatient.

"Is only you in here now?"

"Yep, nobody's here anymore; they all left."

Simone takes out his phone and navigates to his messaging app. He hastily sends a message to his closest friend, Lucian, pouring out his thoughts and feelings in a flurry of texts.

Simone types in:

'Hey Lucian! I hope you're doing well. I just realised that I have some free time, and I was wondering if you would like to spend more time together and catch up on things. I've been looking forward to seeing you, and I would love to chat and tell you all about what's been happening in my life lately.'

After putting his phone back in his jacket pocket, he exits the audition room and walks towards his bike.

The current weather is showing signs of increased turbulence. His phone suddenly alerted him that he had received a message.

'The cafe is just a few blocks away, and I plan to arrive there precisely 20 minutes from now. I'm looking forward to seeing you too.'

Lucian answered.

Simone deftly inserts the key into the lock, twisting it quickly as he frees his bicycle from its secure position. With a determined look in his eyes, as he pushes down on the pedals, he propels himself forward towards the charming cafe nestled in the corner of the next street. His mind eagerly anticipates the moment when he will be enveloped in the tantalising aroma of freshly brewed coffee as he tries to shake off the memories of the rough start to his morning. The memory of missing that audition still haunts him. He can't help but think about how different things could have been if he had just made it on time. The nerves and excitement leading up to it, the sound of his heart pounding in his chest as he walked in, and the disappointment washing over him when he realised, he had missed it - all of these details replay in his mind repeatedly. It's like a movie he can't turn off, and he's stuck in the audience, watching his own life play out before him.

5

Jade is on a mission to discover the tastiest vegan recipes out there! She's glued to her laptop, scouring the internet for mouth-watering plant-based dishes to make her taste, and Simone's buds dance with joy.

"Vegan chickpea curry jacket potatoes"

"Maybe I can try this tonight." She says to herself.

She writes down all the ingredients needed to prepare the meal on another piece of paper.

Four sweet potatoes

coconut oil

1½ tsp cumin seeds

One large onion, diced.

Two garlic cloves, crushed.

thumb-sized piece of ginger, finely grated.

One green chilli, finely chopped.

1 tsp garam masala

1 tsp ground coriander

½ tsp turmeric

2 tbsp tikka masala paste

2 x 400 g can chop tomatoes

2 x 400 g can chickpeas, drained.

Lemon wedges and coriander leaves.

As she finishes jotting down notes with her trusty pen onto a crisp white paper, she carefully places them into her sleek bag and approaches the bathroom.

She takes a deep breath and steps into the shower, feeling the cool tiles under her feet. She reached out her hand and turned the shiny silver faucet, feeling the smooth handle turn quickly in her grip. As the water begins to flow, she adjusts the temperature, gradually turning up the heat until the steam rises around her, enveloping her in a warm, comforting embrace.

As she relished the warmth of the water, time seemed to slip away. After a few minutes of indulging in the shower, she reluctantly turned off the tap and stepped out, feeling refreshed and invigorated.

Jade wraps a long towel around her body, her wet hair dripping, and begins to dress.

She stands in front of the mirror, watching the warm air from the blow dryer tousle her lengthy hair, making it sway gently. With each brush pass, she carefully detangles every strand, relishing the sensation of the bristles gliding through her hair. Finally, satisfied with the results, she reaches out to grab her favourite jacket, feeling the soft fabric under her fingers as she puts it on.

Her footsteps echo softly on the hardwood floor as she turns and heads towards the kitchen. As she enters the room, the brewed coffee and pancake aroma still fills her senses.

As she walks towards the window, her steps are measured and deliberate. Her eyes take in the details of the room, noting the subtle changes in lighting as she moves closer to the source of natural light. She holds onto the hope of seeing the sun. She closed her eyes and imagined casting a warm and inviting glow on her skin, and she paused for a moment to take in the sensation of its imaginable warmth. The window is adorned with intricate designs, etched with great skill into the glass. She runs her fingers over the patterns, carefully tracing the curves and lines. Looking outside, and after opening her eyes, she takes in the view with a sense of appreciation for the small details that make up the vibrant scene before her. The people on the street move with a sense of purpose, each one a unique character in the bustling cityscape. The sounds of cars honking, people chatting, and music playing filter in through the open window, creating a rich tapestry of sensory experience.

Standing by the window, she takes a deep breath, fully immersing herself in the present moment. The rain droplets have just begun to fall, filling the air with calmness and tranquillity. She can smell the dampness of the concrete and the sweet fragrance of the flowers in the garden, mixed with the refreshing aroma of the rainwater. It's as if the rain has awakened her senses, leaving her feeling refreshed and alive.

At the same time...

Simone sits comfortably on a small wooden chair by the window in the coffee shop. He slowly sips his warm, frothy oat latte, enjoying the creamy texture and rich flavour. With a colourful cover, the book in front of him is propped open with an undersized stand. He is completely engrossed in the story, eyes scanning each line intensely. The soft chatter of other patrons and the gentle hum of the espresso machine provide a soothing background to his peaceful reading experience.

He considers texting Jade about what happened but decides to wait until he sees her.

As he approaches the quaint coffee shop, the aroma of baked goods wafting towards him, Lucian takes a deep breath of the crisp morning air. With his towering height and unmistakably Romanian features, he confidently pushes open the door, the bell chiming cheerfully as he steps inside. The cosy interior of the shop greets him with warm lighting and comfortable seating as he spots Simone seated at a table near the window. Their meeting had been arranged the day before, and Lucian couldn't help but feel excited as he made his way over to him.

"How long has it been?" Lucian asks.

Simone turns to his right to meet Lucian's eyes. "Hello, you! Has it been a month or perhaps a little longer since we last spoke?"

Simone stands up from his chair. He takes a few steps towards Lucian, his eyes fixed on him with a soft and welcoming gaze. He wraps his arms around him as he reaches him, pulling him close to his chest. His embrace is warm and tender, and he lingers in the hug for a few moments, savouring the feeling of his body against his.

Over several years, they have developed a powerful bond and maintained a close friendship.

Lucian is a football player in the Dutch second division and recently has been very busy with the start of the new season.

"Yeah, after you met that girl, you disappeared," Lucian laughs.

Simone, smiling back, rebates. "I didn't disappear. You were just busy with your training."

"Yes, you are right! So, tell me about this new girl you mentioned on the phone."

The weather outside is different now! The skies are clearing up, and the sun is peeking through the clouds. The first rays of sunlight pour through the windows where Simone and Lucian are sitting, illuminating the patrons with a delicate and warm glow—the dust particles in the air dance in the light, creating a mesmerising sight. The gentle hum of conversation fills the air as people sip their coffee and tea, taking in the peaceful moment.

A waiter from the coffee shop approaches Lucian and inquires if he needs anything.

"Anything for you?"

"Can you get me some tea? Any, I don't mind. Actually, can I have black tea?" Lucian asks.

"Sure, I'll bring it to you now!"

Simone looks at Lucian, laughing.

"What? Are you sick or something? Wow, I can't believe I've never seen you sipping tea."

"Yes, before you 'disappeared', I developed a habit of drinking too much coffee, which you may have influenced."

"I'm sorry, but I don't think your tea habits will affect me," Simone says.

Suddenly, two young girls catch Lucian's attention and eagerly approach them, their faces beaming excitedly. Without hesitation, they nestle onto the seats beside Simone, making themselves comfortable as they want the guys to start a conversation.

Lucian looks at the girls and then back to Simone.

"It seems like you no longer pay attention to any girl."

Lucian says playfully.

Simone looks around and smiles.

"Every time I gaze at Jade, my heart skips a beat. She is the epitome of beauty, with her flawless complexion, mesmerising eyes, and luscious hair that cascades down her shoulders. But her appeal goes beyond just her physical appearance, you know? There is a certain grace and elegance to how she carries herself, with a poise that exudes confidence and self-assuredness."

As he pauses momentarily, he tries to summon the vivid memories of the past few weeks spent together. The moments that made his heart skip a beat, the laughs they shared, the adventures they embarked on - all rushing back to him in a blur of emotions.

"What I love the most about Jade is her unwavering support and devotion to me. She has been my rock through thick and thin, always there to lift me when I feel low, especially with what's going on with my auditions. Her unwavering loyalty and trust in me have been the driving force behind my success. I am truly blessed to have her as my partner and soulmate."

Simone's eyes glimmered with a warm and radiant light, illuminating her face with joy and contentment.

"She's the girl I always needed next to me."

Lucian smiles at the words he just heard.

"Are you the man she always needed next to her?"

6

Late in the morning, the supermarket's interior is bustling with activity. Customers are busy picking out groceries from the neatly arranged aisles as Jade walks in with a small shopping basket while fresh produce and baked goods fill the air. The bright fluorescent lights illuminate the space, highlighting the vibrant colours of the various products on display. The sound of chatter and carts rolling on the smooth floor creates a lively ambience, making the supermarket exciting.

Jade's focused gaze scans the well-stocked supermarket shelves, her fingers carefully inspecting the vibrant produce and fresh herbs. She carefully selects each ingredient for the meal she envisions, considering each item's texture, colour, and scent.

"Where do they keep the Masala?" She asks herself.

The alluring aroma of exotic spices filled the hallway as she took each step with graceful anticipation.

As Jade turned around, a mysterious figure with luscious dark hair caught her eyes, slowly making their way towards her.

She stands before a spicy shelf, her eyes scanning the surroundings, when she hears a voice in the vicinity and her heart races.

"Hey, Jade! Fancy to meet you here."

She recognises the voice instantly, and her eyes fixate on the direction of the sound. She sees a figure walking towards her, and as he gets closer, she can make out his features. Her mind raced with thoughts of what he might say or do, and she could feel her palms starting to sweat. She takes a deep breath as he approaches her, trying to steady her nerves and prepare herself for what's to come.

"It's not fancy meeting you."

The dark-haired guy, now close to Jade, answers.

"Are you still holding a grudge against me?"

"Are you curious if people still hold a grudge against you?"

As Tiberius approaches Jade, his ex-girlfriend, the 27-year-old Romanian man wraps his arms around her warmly.

As Jade pushed Tiberius away, more and more people passing by stopped in their tracks and gathered around, trying to catch a glimpse of what was happening. The growing crowd caused the situation to become even more tense and uncomfortable for everyone involved.

"Don't... please." Jade's gaze shifts to the individuals encompassing her.

She attempted to ease the worries of those around her by saying, "Don't worry, everything is under control."

With the world gradually returning to normalcy, individuals are beginning to focus on their affairs once again.

"What? Why? I'm just being friendly, is all." Tiberius says.

"No, you're just being a dick now. Can you leave me alone?"

She purposefully lowers her voice to avoid drawing attention from anyone nearby.

"Okay, okay... Again, I want you to know how deeply sorry I am for what happened. Please let me know if I can do anything to make things right."

Jade is now getting impatient.

This time louder, "Can you go? Please."

Jade's face contorted with frustration and anger as she watched Tiberius's retreating figure. She noticed how his broad shoulders tensed with each step, his back straight and determined as he moved further and further away. His footsteps echoed in the empty hallway, the only sound in the tense silence between them. As he vanished around the corner, Jade was annoyed and disappointed, her mind replaying their conversation repeatedly.

"Well, I'm going to do it without Masala..."

With a shopping basket in her hand, she takes a few purposeful strides towards the checkout area, her gaze scanning the shelves for any last-minute purchases. As she arrives at the cash register, she sets down her basket and reaches for her wallet, ready to complete her shopping trip.

As Jade approaches the till, her face is etched with a deep frown of frustration and disappointment.

"Vegan?" Asks the cashier.

"Yes, I've been vegan for the last three years."

As Jade stands at the checkout counter, nervously fidgeting with her purse, the cashier notices her unease and offers her a few reassuring words. The sound of the cashier's voice, filled with genuine concern and kindness, helps to ease Jade's tension and put her at ease. Her muscles relaxed, and her breathing slowed as relief washed over her. The unexpected act of kindness and understanding from a stranger has brought hope and positivity into her day, lifting her spirits and brightening her outlook on life. The genuine empathy this stranger express has left a lasting impression, reminding her that amidst the chaos and struggles of everyday life, there are still good-hearted people who care.

"You look stunning! Your skin is glowing, and I'm just curious - have you noticed any physical or mental changes since becoming vegan?"

"I'm feeling more energetic, I have more focus, and I'm feeling less foggy since becoming vegan."

Says Jade, watching the cashier deftly hand over the food, completing the order with practised ease.

"I'm willing to attempt it and see how it goes. I appreciate the conversation we had. Wishing you a wonderful day ahead! "

"I needed this, too. Thank you." Said Jade, lifting the shopping bags with her.

As she steps out of the supermarket, she meticulously inspects the shopping bags to ensure that they are sturdy enough to carry the weight of the bags all the way home. She chooses the most robust bags available, knowing they will be tested on the long walk back.

7

Lucian and Simone are sitting across from each other. Simone holds his mug of coffee tightly with both hands, taking small, frequent sips as he engages in a deep conversation with Lucian. They were discussing Jade, a topic that seemed to have their undivided attention. Simone spoke sombrely, his eyes focused on Lucian as he shared his thoughts and concerns about Jade in great detail. Lucian listened attentively, occasionally nodding in agreement and interjecting with his own insights.

"Today, I prepare to surprise Jade with something I know will bring her great joy. I feel my excitement building with each passing moment as I carefully plan every detail, from the timing of the surprise to the presentation of the gift. I cannot wait to see her look of pure delight as she discovers what I have in store. But I can't spill the beans yet - she'll have to wait until this evening to find out!"

"What is it?" Lucian asks.

"I'm not going to tell you now!"

"What? Why? It's not for me..."

"Yeah, I know, but..."

"Have you ever felt like someone is keeping something from you? It can be frustrating, right? They claim they have something but are unwilling to share it. That's not fair." Concludes Lucian.

Lucian's heart races with excitement as he skilfully manoeuvres the conversation, feeling a sense of satisfaction as he gradually coaxes Simone into revealing the details of the surprise he has in store for Jade. His expression remains neutral, but his mind is buzzing with anticipation as he listens intently to every word Simone utters, eagerly imagining the exciting possibilities that could lie ahead. Finally, with a sly grin, Lucian feels triumphant as he successfully extracts the information he is seeking, eager to savour the anticipation of what's to come.

"Okay, wait."

Simone reaches into his jacket pocket, feeling the smooth fabric against his fingertips as he retrieves his phone. With a gentle swipe of his thumb, he unlocks the screen and opens the gallery app, eagerly anticipating the images stored within.

"That's what I had for Jade."

As he gazes at his phone screen, his eyes fixate on the image of an adorable Labrador puppy, its fur a luscious golden brown and its eyes big and bright. He can't help but feel a surge of joy as he takes in the sheer cuteness of the little creature.

"Although I am not a fan of dogs, I must admit that this particular one is gorgeous," Lucian says.

"Thank you! Jade spent the last two weeks telling me how badly she wanted a dog, and last week, I went to this doghouse and got him for us."

Lucian's eyes widened in shock as his mouth dropped open in surprise! "Do you guys live together already?"

"Have you ever felt like your life is a movie and you're the main character? That's exactly how I feel when we're together - like we're living out a scene from a romantic movie." Says Simone.

"Wow... never thought of you being this way. Jade had a profound impact on your character and behaviour, and it caused a significant transformation in your personality."

Lucian was surprised at the changes he had observed in Simone's character and behaviour.

"You are now vastly different from who you used to be before encountering Jade, with new perspectives, attitudes, and habits that reflect her influence on your life."

"Suppose I exhibited those particular traits previously, yet I was only required to delve deeper to unearth them? Perhaps they were hidden beneath layers of self-doubt or insecurity, and only after some introspection and personal growth could I fully embody them once again."

After consuming the last sip of coffee, Simone places the empty cup on the table and glances at the time displayed on his phone.

"I'm meeting Jade in thirty minutes, and we plan to visit a library together."

"Okay, sure. I have to go to training anyway. I had such a wonderful time catching up with you, and I don't want to wait any longer to see you again. It would be fantastic to plan a meet-up soon, perhaps over a pizza or something to continue our conversation."

At that moment, Lucian's lips curve upwards into a genuine and friendly smile as he looks towards Simone, conveying a sense of warmth and trust. With a sense of ease and familiarity, Lucian reaches out. He places his hand on Simone's back, providing a solid and encouraging pat that radiates a sense of brotherhood and mutual respect.

"Yes, I agree. I'll pay for the tea; don't worry about that."

"Thank you. I look forward to seeing you soon. Please let me know what she thinks of the dog, okay?"

"I will," Simone answered back.

Lucian steps out of the cosy coffee shop, feeling refreshed and energised by his delicious cup of black tea. As he exits, we notice Simone walking up to the counter to pay the bill with a charming smile. The warm ambience of the coffee shop and the friendly staff made their day brighter and gave them the perfect start to their day.

Once bustling with activity, the cafe now has a noticeably lower volume of customers.

"It's on me. Don't worry about it. How did the audition go?" Asks the barista.

"Thank you so much...Oh no, I messed up big time! I arrived at the wrong time. By the time I got there, everyone had already left. It was such a bummer!"

"Can't you rebook it?" Asks the barista.

"No, I can't rebook it. that's the harsh reality of this job. There are no do-overs or second chances. It's tough, but we have to keep pushing forward."

"Well, hopefully, next time will be different."

"I will make sure it will be."

Simone turns around to the barista and waiters.

As he prepares to depart from the cafe, he casts a warm smile towards every person in the bustling coffee shop, his eyes radiating with a genuine desire to spread joy. "May your day be filled with stunning beauty," he declares with a cheerful tone, his words leaving an uplifting impact on everyone present.

Simone is experiencing a deep sense of love for the first time, as evidenced by his emotions. It's the feeling that arises when you meet your soulmate, *and even if it is only in the initial stage, Simone is confident that Jade is the one for him.*

8

Jade unlocks the front door of her second-floor walk-up flat, her arms loaded with a damp, brown paper bag filled with fresh produce and pantry staples. She steps inside, greeted by the familiar scent of her home: a mix of warm spices, laundry detergent, and a hint of mustiness. She removes her shoes and sets the bag on the scratched wooden kitchen table, clearing away a pile of unopened mail. As she unpacks the groceries, she takes note of the wilted lettuce and bruised apples, making a mental note to eat those first. After putting everything away, she takes a deep breath, feeling grateful to be home after a very intense moment.

Opening the laptop, she presses the power button to turn it on. The screen flickers to life, revealing a familiar desktop background. She eagerly opens her email app, hoping to find some unread messages waiting for her, but her inbox is empty.

Jade texts Simone.

'I'm all set and ready whenever you are. Can't wait to see your beautiful face!'

As Jade focuses on sending Simone a message on her phone, she suddenly becomes aware of a flurry of notifications that demand her attention. She quickly unlocked her phone and saw that Tiberius had sent several apology messages. The messages were repetitive, each expressing regret for his actions and pleading for my forgiveness. The tone of the messages was sad and remorseful, giving off a sense of desperation and guilt.

'I apologise for my actions. Is there a chance for your forgiveness?'

As soon as Jade spots Tiberius's name on her screen, she knows she needs to act. Without hesitation, she reaches for the "block" button, determined to end his constant contact.

She takes deep breaths to prevent anything from ruining the beautiful moment she's having with Simone.

At the same time, the bell rings.

As Jade turned the doorknob, her heart quickened with anticipation. When the door swung open, she was met with the warm smile of Simone. Without hesitation, she wrapped her arms tightly around Simone's shoulders, feeling the comfort of their embrace.

Jade smiles at him.

"I find myself missing you constantly. Can you give me any advice or support on how to cope with this feeling?"

"How about this: I'll be your loyal companion, always by your side. And the best part? I promise never to complain!" Simone answered.

"How was your morning?" He then asks.

Jade walks toward the kitchen again and settles comfortably on the wooden chair at the kitchen table, her fingertips grazing over the smooth surface as she reaches for a bowl of freshly cut apples. She pops a juicy piece into her mouth, savouring the sweetness on her tongue as she takes in the vibrant colours of the assorted apples before her.

"A very long morning...I went to the shop to create a new vegan meal for us."

Simone's eyes sparkle as he reaches for a crisp, juicy apple. He takes a bite, savouring the sweetness of the fruit.

"Oh, yes? What's the name of the meal?"

"I won't tell you. You will try it and see what you think."

Simone closes the distance between himself and Jade, his heart racing with anticipation as he leans in and presses his lips against Jade's, savouring the softness and warmth of the kiss.

"I can't help but love you, Jade. Your creativity never ceases to amaze me!"

As Jade's mind wandered, she recollected the events that had occurred earlier.

"And my dog died..."

"How? When?" Simone asks.

Jade raises the apple to her lips, admiring its vibrant colour and glossy sheen before biting. As her teeth penetrate the firm flesh, she feels a rush of juice flood her mouth, carrying the fruit's sweet and tangy taste. However, her momentary joy is quickly replaced by a profound melancholy that creeps into her expression, as if eating the apple has unlocked a trove of memories and emotions that she had long buried within her.

"My mum called me a couple of hours ago and gave me the news."

"I'm sorry to hear that, babe. Will she be getting another one?"

"I am sure she wouldn't want to be alone," Jade answers.

With slow, deliberate movements, Jade places the shiny red apple on the pristine white plate, careful not to leave a blemish. She then walks towards Simone, her footsteps echoing softly on the polished marble floor.

"How did the audition go?"

As Simone listened to Jade's morning account, which was filled with events and emotions, he decided to remain silent rather than offer comments or opinions.

"I feel like it went pretty well! You know how nerve-wracking auditions can be, but I gave it my all and feel good about it."

"When are they going to let you know if you succeed?" Jade asks.

Simone reaches for his phone, feeling its familiar weight in his hand as he unlocks the screen and navigates to his calendar app.

"Soon, I hope..."

He gazes at Jade, seemingly eager to steer the conversation in a different direction.

"Ready to go?" Simone kisses her on the forehead.

"Yes, let me change my bag."

Jade enters the room and immediately begins reorganising their belongings. With purposeful movements, they transfer each item from a smaller bag to a larger one. The sound of rustling fabric fills the air as Jade works meticulously, ensuring every item finds its proper place in the new bag.

9

Simone and Jade stroll down the street, their hands intertwined, admiring every adorable building they encounter.

As they gaze upwards, they notice that the once cloudy sky has now transformed into a breathtaking shade of blue, with a scattering of white and grey, fluffy clouds that seem to be floating effortlessly across the horizon. The gusts of wind blowing through the air are strong enough to make the trees sway back and forth, and they can feel their hair whipping around their face as they take in the refreshing scent of fresh air. The leaves rustle loudly as they dance to the rhythm of the wind, creating a soothing melody that echoes throughout the surroundings.

Just now, Jade remembers Simone had to meet with Lucian.

"Did you meet Lucian?"

"Yes, we met after the audition. However, he had to rush out for his training session. I wish we could have spent more time together."

As Jade looks on, her mouth curves upwards into a warm and welcoming smile, lighting up her entire face with a joyous glow.

"Have you told him that you watch all of his matches?" Jade asks.

"Nah, I was too busy talking about you..."

"What did you say about me?"

The sky is covered by a dense, dark layer of grey clouds, which block the sun's rays and cast a gloomy ambience onto the surroundings. Once brimming with life, the trees shed their leaves, leaving the branches barren and exposed. The leaves that fall to the ground create a beautiful and intricate pattern, a mixture of warm colours like red, yellow, and orange. The branches sway back and forth, and the leaves rustle, creating a soothing sound that echoes through the air.

Simone notices that Jade's hands are cold and places her hand gently inside his pocket to keep her warm. She feels the warmth of his pocket and the gentle touch of his hand and smiles gratefully at him.

"I told him that you are fantastic and unique. And that maybe you were the girl I needed to meet to bring out my best."

Jade playfully reacts to the word "maybe".

"Maybe? I am the girl that brings out the best of you."

She starts tickling him…

"Say the opposite. Come on… I'd fight you…" said Jade, smiling.

"Yeah, you are right." Reply Simone.

"Can we go in there one moment?" He then asks.

As they stroll along, Simone's sharp eye catches sight of a quaint yet elegant boutique with an impeccable selection of classic, timeless watches.

They enter the shop slowly to appreciate the interior colours and antique aroma.

As they walked into the small antique watch store, they were immediately struck by the cosy interior. The walls were lined with shelves and display cases filled with vintage timepieces of all shapes and sizes. The gentle ticking of the clocks provided a soothing background sound, and the warm lighting accentuated the intricate details of the watches. It was a charming and intimate space, perfect for any horology enthusiast.

Simone noticed an old-fashioned watch.

"Have you ever wondered about the magic in creating something as unique as this?"

"They explain it here," Jade says.

Jade starts reading out loud.

"Watches were developed in the 17th century from spring-powered clocks, which appeared as early as the 14th century. During most of its history, the watch was a mechanical device driven by clockwork, powered by winding a mainspring, and keeping time with an oscillating balance wheel. These are called mechanical watches."

"That's very interesting." Exclaims Simone.

"I had no idea you had such a strong interest in watches."

Simone's index finger lingers on the elegant timepiece's small, rectangular price tag, which displays the price in bold, black letters against a crisp white background.

His eyes narrow slightly as she contemplates the cost, weighing the luxurious features of the watch against her budget.

"Ever since I realised how expensive it is to check the time…"

As the joke unfolded, they both burst into uncontrollable laughter, their bodies shaking with amusement.

"You are terrible."

"You are beautiful."

They share a kiss before leaving the store together.

As they exit the store, an eerie silence falls between them and the staff; nothing is uttered.

Despite the sun shining brightly, its warmth is still not enough to overcome the piercing chill of the wind. The trees sway vigorously as if dancing to the tune of the gusts. The grass blades are flattened, struggling to stand tall against the forceful breeze. The air is filled with rustling leaves and the occasional creaking of branches. The frigid wind seems to have no mercy, stinging exposed skin and challenging breathing.

"So, where is the library you mentioned?"

"I need to check on the map, but it shouldn't be that far."

"Can we stop for a coffee?" Simone asks.

"Watch out; soon enough, you might not be able to get your favourite coffee fix from your go-to coffee shops anymore. They might ban you for being too much of a coffee addict!"

They both share a laugh.

Jade takes the lead for once. "Can we try a new one today?"

"We can try anything, but it's your responsibility if it's not good."

The two halts in front of a quaint cafe that appears different from the others they have passed by. The cafe's exterior is adorned with vibrant flowers, and the smell of freshly brewed coffee wafts through the air, enticing the senses: Back to Black is the shop's name.

"The name sounds intriguing…" says Jade.

"Let's try it out," Simone says.

As they step through the glass door of the coffee shop, the warm, earthy aroma of fresh coffee greets them, mingling with the nutty scent of roasted coffee beans. The walls are lined with shelves stocked with various coffee blends, and the colourful chalkboard menu above the barista's counter lists an array of beverages. The inviting atmosphere and the promise of a delicious cup of coffee make it impossible to resist the urge to stay and indulge in a moment of pure bliss.

"Wow," Simone exclaimed.

"Close your eyes," says Simone to Jade.

"Let's try something fun! Try to close your eyes for a brief moment and let your mind wander. "

"Oh, nice, yes, I can try."

"Ready?"

"Okay, eyes closed."

"The scent of freshly brewed coffee is truly heavenly! Can you recall when the aroma filled your senses, leaving you feeling invigorated and ready to tackle the day? And if you're a coffee lover like me, have you ever imagined tying the knot with a coffee bean, enchanted by its rich flavour and aroma? It's a thought that has crossed my mind more than once!"

As Jade opened her eyes, she swiftly jabbed him in the shoulder.

"You are cheating on me already," Jade says playfully.

"It's coffee beans, Jade."

As Simone and Jade continue conversing right at the entryway, customers have no choice but to wait for them to move away. The delay is causing some dissatisfaction among the customers, who are growing impatient with the situation.

"Oh my god, sorry…"

As they both burst into laughter, they make their way towards the till with a spring in their step, eagerly anticipating what's to come.

Simone confidently steps forward, anticipating Jade's desire for a warm cup of coffee. He takes the lead and quickly places an order for them both.

"Can I please get one oat cappuccino and one oat latte in a takeaway cup?"

The barista leaned over the counter with a smile and asked, "What kind of coffee can I brew up for you today?"

"Amore? Which one would you like?" Asks Simone to Jade.

"I'm excited to learn more about the one from Guatemala! Can you tell me more about it?" Asks Jade to the barista.

The friendly barista brings out a beautifully designed brochure from behind the counter. The brochure is meticulously crafted and lists various coffee types available, complete with detailed descriptions and brewing methods. They can't help but feel impressed by the attention to detail and the passion for coffee that this establishment exudes.

"You can find all of them here as all the juicy details about that exquisite coffee you were asking about. You don't want to miss out on this one!"

"Oh wow!"

"Too many different types," exclaimed Jade.

The café offers a wide variety of coffee beans worldwide.

The brochure vividly portrays the rich and complex flavour profile of Guatemalan coffee, delving into its unique aroma and notes of acidity.

"How about we give Guatemalans a shot? I've heard fantastic things about it. I want to try it!"

"Okay," Simone answers.

"Can we please have both with the Guatemalan coffee?"

With its rustic decor and warm lighting, the cosy little cafe is abuzz with activity as patrons bustle about, chatting, laughing, and savouring their beverages. The aroma of freshly brewed coffee fills the air, enticing the senses and making one's mouth water. Amidst this lively atmosphere, Simone and Jade stand in a long queue that snakes behind them, patiently waiting their turn to get the coffee. The line seems to be moving at a snail's pace, but they don't mind, as they are engrossed in conversation, catching up on each other's lives and enjoying the cafe's ambience.

Simone and Jade get the coffee and sit by the window on one of the small tables.

"How is it?" Simone asks.

As she sips the coffee, she is immediately hit with the bold and robust flavour that lingers on her tongue. However, as she continues to savour it, she detects a subtle but distinct taste of exquisite chocolate that subtly dances with the caramel notes, creating an exquisite balance of flavours that is both indulgent and satisfying.

"This coffee is truly a masterpiece, crafted with the finest ingredients and blended to perfection; I love it." Says Jade.

"Better than the one I do at home?"

Jade couldn't contain her laughter as it erupted with infectious joy.

"Your coffee is a masterpiece that no one can ever replicate. It's unique, just like you."

Simone's deep brown eyes light up with delight as a broad smile spread across his face, revealing pearly white teeth. He extends his hand towards Jade, gently intertwining his fingers with hers and giving a reassuring squeeze as if to convey a sense of comfort and security. The touch of their hands creates a subtle spark, igniting a sense of connection between them.

"I have a surprise for you," Simone says, holding Jade's hand.

"Do you? Really?"

"Unfortunately, you'll have to wait a little longer. The good news is that it won't be too long! You can expect it this evening."

"I can sense that you have something on your mind that you can't keep to yourself."

Simone sits comfortably in his chair, his hands wrapped around the warm ceramic cup of his oat latte, as he leans in to listen to Jade with rapt attention.

"Sure, but we'll have to wait regardless. Additionally, we have to visit the library first."

"Shall we go now?"

"Yes. I was thinking of going for a nice walk."

They slowly push themselves up from the comfortable chairs, their muscles stretching as they rise to their feet. They take their first steps towards the exit, their eyes focused on the door at the end of the room. The soles of their shoes make a soft thud against the polished wooden floor, echoing through the spacious room. As they walk, their movements become more purposeful and confident, their strides lengthening with each passing moment. Finally, they reach the door and grasp the handle, the cool metal shattering down their spine.

As Simone sees the soft and slow footsteps of an elderly woman approaching, he quickly moves towards the door to open it for her. He notices that the woman's hair is white as snow, and her wrinkled face is adorned with a gentle smile. Simone greets her warmly, and as he holds the door open, he says, "Please, let me help you." The elderly woman nods and thanks him before slowly making her way inside.

"Thank you, young boy." Says the old lady.

"Don't worry."

Despite being in her seventies, the elderly woman's appearance and demeanour are strikingly youthful and energetic. Her clear skin and vibrant eyes suggest a healthy lifestyle, while her quick movements and confident posture indicate strength and agility. It is as if the passage of time has had little effect on her, and she continues to exude a youthful spirit that defies her age.

She quickly turns towards Jade.

"Is he your boyfriend?"

Jade looks at Simone, smiling.

"As far as I know, yes."

"Wow, you made a fantastic choice by picking this guy! You've picked an absolute gem!"

The elderly woman shuffles away with slow, deliberate steps towards the dimly lit bar, her gnarled hand gripping tightly onto the handle of her cane as she goes.

10

As the clock strikes twelve, the sun reaches its zenith, casting a bright glow over everything in sight. The wind that was once howling fiercely has now died down to a gentle breeze, causing the leaves on the trees to sway rhythmically. The air is crisp and refreshing, and the sound of chirping birds can be heard in the distance, adding to the moment's tranquillity.

"Coffee beans before and old lady after, Mr. Svanera, you are not doing well."

Simone laughs and quickly grabs your hand, holding it tightly as if you both shared a hilarious inside joke.

"It brings me immense joy and admiration when you communicate your feelings of jealousy towards me in a genuine and heartfelt way. Your words can make me feel loved and valued, and I appreciate your effort to express yourself meaningfully."

Simone and Jade strolled together; their fingers intertwined; Simone's phone suddenly erupted with persistent vibrations.

Simone gazes up at the bright screen of his phone, pondering whether to answer the call from the unknown number or ignore it completely. His mind races with curiosity and uncertainty as he debates the possible outcomes of his decision.

Jade hesitates.

Simone's heart skipped a beat as he heard the voice on the other end of the phone. He immediately recognised it and felt a rush of emotions.

The call is about the surprise he has for Jade.

As he walks away from Jade, he turns his back to her to hide the excitement and nervousness that he feels inside. His heart beats faster as he listens to what the person on the phone says.

"Excuse me for a moment, Jade," Simone says, looking back at her with a reassuring glance before turning his attention back to the call.

Simone tries to distance himself so she cannot listen.

"Yes. Is it all good?"

"Hi, I just wanted to remind you that everything is ready for you to pick up the dog this evening around 19:00."

"Okay, I'll be coming there with my girlfriend."

Simone's voice has a notably deeper and more subdued tone than what is typical for him.

Standing a few meters away, Jade strains her ears to catch Simone's words, but her efforts prove futile.

"See you soon." Says Simone, ending the call.

Jade's lips are curved upwards in a smile, but her expression also reveals a sense of curiosity. "May I know who that was?" she asks inquisitively.

"The casting director called me, and they want to see me again."

"Oh, that's fantastic news."

Jade hugged Simone and shared every bit of joy with him.

"They just want to see me again...But yeah, that's good news."

"After visiting the library, we plan to have a drink to celebrate."

As soon as Jade stops walking, she pulls out her smartphone and unlocks it. She opens the map application with a few taps and searches for the library's location.

She inserts Rijksmuseum Library on the map.

"The app says it will take 31 minutes to walk and 9 minutes if we take the bus."

"Can we walk? It's not that cold yet." Says Simone.

Jade's eyes lit up as she looked at Simone. "Is it still not cold enough for you?" she asked, taking Simone's hands. "Wow, your hands are freezing!" she chuckled, rubbing them to warm them up.

"Cold hands, warm heart" answered Simone, smiling.

As they shared a good laugh, they started walking towards the library, fully aware that the journey would take considerable time. They admired the beauty of their surroundings, taking in the sights and sounds of the bustling city streets as they made their way to their destination.

"What is your biggest fear?" Asks Simone.

"My biggest fear? I think the thought of falling short of the life I've always envisioned for myself."

"And what plans do you have for the near future? I'm curious to know more!" Asks Simone again.

"Right now, I'm just thinking of doing everything I want. To make every moment count. What is your biggest fear?"

Simone stops looking at Jade and turns towards the tall buildings.

His muscles involuntarily contract, causing his body to stiffen. He gazes around the street, carefully scrutinising every detail of his surroundings. His mind races as he searches for the perfect words to express his thoughts, carefully weighing each to ensure their accuracy and impact.

Deep in thought, Simone pauses for a moment before turning to Jade. "Have you ever considered the impact you'll have on the world long after you're gone?" she asks. Jade looks up at him, intrigued. "For me, it's not just about achieving success or personal goals," Simone continues. "It's about making a positive difference and leaving the world in a better state than I found it. That's the legacy I want to leave behind." Jade nods, impressed by Simone's determination to make a lasting impact.

"It's my biggest fear that I won't be able to achieve that."

"Wow, that's deep. Do you think it's possible to do that?" Asks jade.

Simone nods in agreement with Jade, adding, "Also, I couldn't agree more about what you said. There's something about living in the present moment that makes life feel more vibrant and alive. Regrets or worries about the future do not weigh you down. Instead, you're fully present and engaged with the world's beauty. You notice things you might otherwise miss - the colours of the sky at sunset, the sound of the wind rustling through the trees, the feel of the sun on your skin. It's a truly enriching way to live."

Simone feels a reassuring squeeze as Jade grips his hand a little tighter.

Simone turns to Jade and poses a thought-provoking question, "Have you ever stopped to ponder on the fact that you are currently existing in this very moment? Does it not make you feel empowered and in control?" *Simone's words evoke a sense of awe and wonder, highlighting the sheer magnificence of the present moment.*

Jade agrees with Simone's statement and compliments his eloquence, saying, "I agree. Well-spoken."

"I'm curious. What made you decide to become an actor in the first place? I don't think we've talked about that yet."

"After Covid struck three years ago, I had much spare time and solitude. It was during this period that I discovered my passion for acting. As I spent more time alone, I became more reflective and creative, and I strongly desired to communicate powerful messages to people. Using my acting talents to achieve this goal became increasingly appealing, and I knew I had to pursue this path."

Jade's heart swells with warmth and joy as she basks in the glow of Simone's beautiful and heartfelt words.

"Do you believe it was destiny?" Jade asks.

"What? A destiny that we met?"

"Yes, what do you think?"

"I may not know everything, but I do know that being with you brings me immense joy. I appreciate that you respect my need for silence and enjoy spending time with you. We deeply understand each other, which fills me with contentment. Your calm and compassionate nature draws me towards you. I feel grateful to have you as my partner, and the most important thing I want to express is my love for you. To answer your question, yes, I believe it was destiny."

As Jade experiences a moment of happiness, the muscles in her face contract, causing the corners of *her mouth to turn upward, gradually stretching her lips into a broad and joyful grin.*

"Have you always been that romantic?"

"Do you believe that I possess romantic qualities?"

"Maybe."

11

The moment's tranquillity was palpable as they walked in silence, taking in the beauty of their surroundings. As they gazed into the distance, they were drawn to the magnificent library, its towering structure imposing yet inviting. The intricate details of its architecture were now visible, from the ornate carvings adorning the columns to the delicate tracery on the windows. The more they looked, the more they were struck by the sheer grandeur of this magnificent building.

The library is impressive from the outside with its grand size and beautiful architecture. However, to *truly appreciate its wonders, they must step inside and see its vast collection of books and resources. The space is well-organised from the outside, inviting, and perfect for those seeking knowledge and inspiration.*

As they approach the entrance, the double door's part ways with a whoosh, allowing them to enter the spacious lobby. A burly security guard, dressed in a crisp uniform, stands at the ready, his hair neatly combed and his eyes scanning the surroundings for potential threats. He greets them with a friendly smile and a polite nod as they approach him, making them feel welcome and safe.

Simone and Jade make their way towards the entrance of the library, their footsteps echoing throughout the quiet corridor. As they approach the first set of doors, they reciprocate the greeting before continuing towards the second set of doors, each taking in the surroundings of the grand library with a sense of wonder and excitement.

"Can I check your bag, Miss?" Asked the security guy.

"Of course."

Jade hands her bag to him.

The security personnel conduct a brief inspection and then gestures to indicate that the area is secure and that the individuals are cleared to proceed without any issues.

Simone and Jade entered the premises.

"Do you know you can read a book while walking through the library?"

"that's exciting." Says Simone.

As they enter the library, the soft glow of the warm lights and the familiar scent of old books immediately envelop them. The quiet hum of rustling pages and hushed whispers create a peaceful ambience that soothes Simone and Jade's souls. The towering shelves filled with literary treasures beckon them, promising hours of exploration and discovery.

Simone turns to Jade and asks her to pause momentarily and imagine returning to relive the experience of reading a book all over again. He wants Jade to think deeply and carefully about which book she would choose to revisit, perhaps savouring the anticipation and excitement of rediscovering a beloved story.

"Think accurately. What books would you reread right now, in this moment?"

"Nice question! Currently, I have a strong desire to reread the book "The Alchemist" by Pablo Coelho."

"I adore that book! It's one of my all-time favourites." Simone exclaimed.

Jade is surprised.

"Do you know we have it at home?"

"No, I don't remember you telling me. I want to reread it, too."

"You will."

She kisses him.

"Let's walk around." Says Jade.

"All right, here is an idea. This library has an enormous collection of books, and it would be great if we could cover as much ground as possible. How about we divide and conquer? We can each explore different sections independently for the next couple of hours and then reconvene here in exactly two hours from now." Proposed Simone.

It looks like Jade is really into the idea!

"What do you think?"

"Sounds like a plan, Batman!"

Their lips met in a gentle kiss that lingered for a moment before they separated, each going their way.

Jade walks down the aisle, touching every book that catches her eye. She pauses occasionally to *pick up a few books and admire their titles as if they were the most stunning objects she had ever seen.*

Jade took out her Air Pods and put on her favourite song, "I'd Rather Go Blind" by Etta James.

As she keeps walking, she is greeted by the warm and inviting ambience of the cosy interior. The space has rows of tall wooden bookshelves, each housing hundreds of books on various topics. The scent of ageing paper and leather bindings fills the air, creating a sense of nostalgia and awe. Soft lighting illuminates the space, casting a warm glow over the rows of books and comfortable reading nooks. This is a place of solace and contemplation, where one can lose oneself in the pages of a novel or dive deep into a research project. Jade is lost in music as she dances and walks until she's captivated by the book she's always wanted to read: "This Time Tomorrow" by Emma Straub.

She takes the book from the shelf, delicately handling it like a fragile treasure. With a gentle flip, she opens it randomly, revealing the yellowed pages within. The aroma of ancient paper and ink fills her nostrils, evoking memories of quiet afternoons lost in a good story. As she inhales deeply, she feels transported to another time and place, where the only thing that matters is the world within the pages of a book.

"That's a fantastic book!"

When Jade hears the voice, a wave of familiarity washes over her as if she has heard it countless times before.

"Are you following me?"

"I could ask the same thing." Answers Tiberius.

"I'm here with my boyfriend, Tiberius."

"I don't see anyone."

"He's--"

Jade shifts her gaze to the other side, craning her neck to glimpse Simone amidst the crowd. However, her surroundings are filled with people *leisurely walking about and immersing themselves in their literary adventures, leaving Jade with nothing but a sense of disappointment.*

Tiberius, noticing that Jade had blocked him, reached out to her with an intent to resolve the issue by proposing to meet her at a place of her convenience. He hoped this would help ease tensions between them and clear the air.

"I noticed that you blocked me, and I wanted to reach out and meet you somewhere to resolve this." For a moment, Jade's patience wanes.

"The issue here is you. You cheated on me, you fucked someone else, You ruined everything we had. You messed up, and I suggest that you make peace with yourself and fuck off."

Suddenly, a booming voice echoed through the library, causing every person in the aisle to snap their heads in its direction. All eyes were fixed on Jade and Tiberius, and the previously quiet atmosphere was shattered.

"Now, can you leave me alone?" Says Jade in a calmer manner.

"Why don't you just listen to me for a few seconds? I want to show you--"

Jade intercepts Tiberius.

"No, I asked you to leave me alone," Jade repeated, this time louder.

"I'm going… bye, Jade…"

12

At the same time...

Simone's footsteps echoed softly on the polished floor as he strolled through the library's aisles. Suddenly, he sees the audiobook section nestled cosily between the bookshelves. He can't resist the temptation and approaches it, eager to peruse the collection. With each step, his anticipation grows, wondering what tales and stories lay ahead.

"Happy Place by Emily Henry. "

"I like the title."

Simone puts the headphones on and presses 'play'.

'Harriet and Wyn have been the perfect couple since they met in college—they go together like salt and pepper, honey and tea, lobster and rolls. Except, for reasons they're still not discussing— they don't.'

The audiobook has completely captivated him now.

Simone closes his eyes and tries to focus solely on listening.

"I have listened to that book two times already."

Lost in his thoughts and unaware of his surroundings, Simone initially fails to register the girl's words. He assumes that the girl must be addressing someone else, not him, and continues listening, oblivious to the potential significance of what he has just heard.

"Do you come here often?"

Simone becomes aware that nobody is responding to the situation, and he starts to think that the words might be related to him.

Simone opened his eyes and turned to his right, where he could hear the girl's voice.

"Are you talking to me?"

"Yes. You are listening to "Happy Place.""

"Yes, I was drawn to the title and decided to listen."

Their silence was thick with unspoken tension as they stood facing each other. The once relaxed and easy-going atmosphere had dissipated into an awkward and uncomfortable one, with the two individuals avoiding eye contact and fidgeting nervously. Every breath felt heavy with unspoken words and emotions, as if a weight had settled over the entire space, leaving a palpable sense of unease. The woman, approximately 25 years old, appears beautiful with blonde hair, blue eyes, and noticeable red lipstick.

"So, do you come here often?"

Simone chooses to continue the discussion.

"Today is special for my girlfriend and me as we ventured into this place for the first time!"

"That's fantastic. Have you lost her already?"

Simone's eyes dart around, surveying his environment in a desperate attempt to catch even the slightest hint of her presence.

"I told her it would have been nice to visit the library individually to focus more on the surroundings."

"That's a great idea! Even though I visit often, I haven't explored the whole library yet. It's so vast."

After being momentarily distracted, Simone focuses on his audiobook and immerses himself again in the story. He adjusts his posture, settles more comfortably, and resumes playback, eager to continue where he left off.

"Can I listen to it with you?" Simone hears in the background.

"Didn't you listen to it already?"

Simone experiences a sudden realisation that the words he had spoken only moments ago were impolite and inappropriate. The gravity of the situation dawns on him as he contemplates the impact of his words and the possible repercussions. His mind races as he tries to think of ways to make amends and rectify the situation.

"Sorry if my behaviour came across as rude. You're fun and engaging to talk to, but I realised you have been a bit too flirty. I hope we can keep up the conversation, but I also want to make sure you respect that I have a girlfriend."

The girl burst into a laugh, showing a bit of nervousness.

"I completely understand how you feel. I have a boyfriend, too."

Simone's lips curved upwards, forming a gentle smile that spread to his cheeks.

"Sorry, I didn't mean --"

"Hey, don't worry, sometimes, it may seem like I'm being flirty… but I'm not."

Abruptly and without warning, she twisted her body to face the opposite direction and reverted to Simone as if a switch had been flipped. The movement was so sudden that it left no opportunity for anyone to anticipate her actions.

"Come with me. I want to show you one cool thing." The girl says, bringing Simone's hands.

Jade strolls through the bookshelves, her eyes scanning the spines of the books as she tries to find the one, she is looking for. She is deep in thought, lost in her own world, and wholly absorbed in her search. Her movements are deliberate and focused, as if trying to find something meaningful. Despite the noise of other people talking and the sound of pages turning, she seems utterly unaware of her surroundings, as if nothing else matters but the book she is searching for.

Jade stops as she sees the e-book section.

She first notices "The Secret, Book & Scone Society by Ellery Adams."

She begins reading the book but quickly puts it away when she realises, she can't focus. She sees something away from her:

The girl led Simone to a section close to the e-book aisle, with Simone following behind without knowing their destination.

She shows Simone the new books she found and expresses her excitement.

"Have you ever had the pleasure of reading this book? Trust me, it's a real page-turner!"

She picks up "The Adventures of Huckleberry Finn" by Mark Twain.

"No, never... what is it about?"

"It exposes the hypocrisy of slavery and demonstrates how racism distorts the oppressors as much as it does those oppressed.'

"Would you say that reading it is worthwhile?" Simone asks.

"Absolutely, yes, also because--"

As Simone stands with his back turned, Jade approaches him from behind, her footsteps silent as she moves closer to Simone's shoulder. The sudden appearance of Jade takes Simone by surprise, causing him to turn around quickly.

The palpable tension in the air is almost suffocating, and it's clear that something significant is about to happen.

"Hey, baby... you, okay?" Jade asks

Simone looked at Jade with surprise but spoke calmly.

"Hey, amore."

Simone takes a small step forward, closing the distance between himself and Jade. With a graceful motion, he leans in and presses his lips gently against Jade's cheek, leaving behind a fleeting yet tender kiss. The moment passes quickly, but the warmth of the gesture lingers in the air.

"She was..."

Then suddenly turn to the girl. "I just realised something - I didn't catch your name yet. What's your name?"

"You seem to have forgotten my name already."

The girl's tone was laced with disappointment and frustration.

Simone's eyes widen with shock, his mouth slightly agape in disbelief.

"Is she your girlfriend?" Asked the girl again.

"No, I don't think I ever asked for your name... and yes, she is my girlfriend..."

Jade Intercede:

"Nice to meet you; I'm Jade."

Simone's eyes meet the girl's, standing before him with a furrowed brow and a look of intense anger. The girl's body language suggests that she is deeply upset by something, as her fists are clenched tightly by her sides and her jaw tenses.

Jade's gaze fixated on the girl as she began to notice her peculiar behaviour. The girl seemed to be moving unsteadily and unpredictably, making Jade uneasy. She couldn't quite pinpoint what was causing this restlessness, but she knew something was amiss.

"You didn't tell me you had a girlfriend."

Simone's facial features suddenly shift as his eyebrows rise, and his eyes widen in response to the realisation that he has mentioned Jade's name in the conversation.

"I did. I also told you that you seemed flirty, and you said you had a boyfriend."

Simone shifts his weight nervously as he turns to Jade, his eyes darting back and forth as if searching for the right words. He takes a deep breath and opens his mouth to speak, but instead, he looks at her, hoping she can see the truth in his eyes. His palms are sweaty, and his heart is racing as he tries to convey his innocence through his body language, standing up straight and keeping his hands at his sides to show that he has nothing to hide.

"And I do recall mentioning my girlfriend to you," Simone responds, trying to clarify the situation.

Jade steps into the conversation to diffuse the situation.

"It's not a big deal. I'm sure you didn't understand each other." Jade intervenes.

Jade has always been a person who prefers to steer clear of any situations that may lead to conflicts or create unnecessary tension and maintains a calm and composed demeanour in all circumstances.

Simone's tone was getting agitated as he responded, "Hold on, I'm confused. Why are you saying that? I've been very clear with you. You approached me and flirted, but I told you to stop because I have a girlfriend. Please, let's stop with the nonsense."

Jade's unease grows with each passing moment, especially as they become more aware of the gazes of the individuals around them. The scrutiny from the crowd is starting to make them feel uneasy and self-conscious.

"Why don't we explore some other place?" Jade asks with a hint of disappointment in her voice.

"Yeah."

As Jade and Simone leave, their fading footsteps echo through the busy library, leaving the young girl feeling abandoned and vulnerable amid the desolate surroundings.

13

"What do you say if we reschedule for another time? That way, we can ensure we have all the time we need to make the most of it, and this time we stick together." Jade asks.

After a long and winding journey filled with ups and downs, Jade has finally arrived at a place where the bond between her and Simone has grown into an unbreakable trust. Jade's trust in Simone is a surface-level feeling and a deep conviction earned through many shared good and bad experiences. Simone has consistently shown himself to be a reliable and supportive partner, and Jade now feels completely secure knowing that Simone has her back, no matter what challenges may arise. This trust has been hard-earned, but it has also brought a sense of peace and contentment to Jade's life that she never thought possible.

"Would you like to grab a coffee somewhere around here?"

"Yes, please, a new coffee Shop?" Simone asks, feeling still a bit tense.

As they take each step, their hands remain at their sides, no longer interlocked as they were before. The sound of their footsteps echoes softly as they walk side by side. Simone seems to be experiencing lingering emotional distress as a result of the recent incident, and his mood and behaviour reflect this. Despite Jade's understanding of what just happened, he appears to be still upset and troubled by the situation, and her demeanour suggests that she is struggling to cope with his feelings.

"Can you just let it go? Please? Trust me, sometimes it's better to move on. What do you think?"

Simone smiles, but she still appears unconvinced.

"I'll try. I promise."

As they leisurely walked along the winding path, their eyes caught sight of a quaint coffee shop that sat nestled next to the calm and peaceful river. The charming little establishment was adorned with rustic wooden shutters and a quaint sign that read, "River's Edge Cafe". The surroundings were simply idyllic: the sound of the water gently lapping against the riverbank, the warm sun glistening on the water's surface, and birds chirping in the nearby trees. They couldn't help but feel the urge to stop and soak it all in as the picturesque scene seemed to transport them to another world of tranquillity and unspoiled beauty.

"Can we sit outside?"

"Let's see the inside one moment."

As they entered the cafe, Simone and Jade quickly scanned the room for an empty table, noticing the colourful artwork on the walls and the warm glow of the pendant lights hanging from the ceiling.

"Wow, it's jam-packed in here. Can you take a seat outside? I'll grab the coffee for both of us."

"Cow milk cappuccino for you, right?"

"You truly have a great sense of humour. You should consider a comedy career!" Jade said sarcastically.

Jade steps through the doorway and scans the outdoor seating area, her eyes settling on the perfect table. She goes over to it, taking in the ambience as she goes.

Simone takes a few steps towards the counter, his footsteps echoing on the tiled floor. As he approaches, he catches the aroma of coffee and the sound of milk being steamed. He greets the barista with a warm smile, his eyes crinkling at the corners.

"Please, can I have an oat cappuccino and oat latte in a takeaway cup?"

The barista behind the counter seems struggling to keep up with the high volume of customers, as evidenced by their hurried movements and constant glances at the long queue. Simone notices that the barista's welcoming facial expression is less inviting than he usually experiences. The tone of the barista's voice is now curt, which seems to be a result of the stressful situation they find themselves in.

"It's 6 euro and 20 pence." The barista says.

"Thank you."

Simone grabs the coffee and walks out of the coffee shop.

Under the almost clear blue sky stands a sturdy wooden table, its surface weathered by the natural elements over time. It is placed on a small patch of green grass by the gently flowing river, which mirrors the surrounding trees and bushes. The calm weather has brought a sense of peace to the area, allowing the chirping birds and the rustling leaves to be the only sounds that break the silence. The cool breeze carries the fresh scent of the wildflowers, making it an ideal spot to sit and relax.

"That's for you, babe..."

"Thank you."

Simone is eager to resume the conversation and delve deeper into the details of the incident in the library, perhaps to understand better what happened and why.

"Do you believe me?"

"Should I?" Answers Jade, smiling at Simone.

"I'm kidding. Of course, I know you don't want to be without me."

Simone's face is contorted with worry, and his leg incessantly bounces up and down. Sensing his distress, she leans in and places her hand on his leg, feeling the tension in his muscles. The warmth of her touch and the gentle pressure of her hand send a message of comfort and support to Simone, who slowly begins to relax and breathe more easily. She keeps her hand on his leg, feeling the subtle changes in his body language and adjusting her touch accordingly until she senses that he has calmed down and is ready to face the challenge.

"Thank you."

"For what?" Jade replies.

Simone leans closer to Jade, the soft light of the white clouds reflecting in their eyes as he stares intently at Jade's gaze. Gradually, a sense of calmness washes over Simone like a gentle wave, settling the fluttering of her heart and soothing the racing of her mind.

"You have this fantastic ability to uplift me at ease. You have a magical power to bring out the best in me. Thank you for being you!"

"I love you, Simone."

As they take their first sip of the steaming hot coffee, the rich aroma fills their senses, and they both can't help but let out a contented sigh.

"I'm blown away by how amazing this coffee is! It's no wonder this shop is packed with people."

The shop is a hive of activity, with a ceaseless procession of customers entering and exiting its doors. The air is filled with overlapping voices, each vying for attention in animated conversations. Some patrons are huddled in small clusters, discussing their purchases, while others are busy scanning the counter filled with pastries and sweets and searching for their desired items. The sights and sounds of the cafe's outside create a lively and bustling atmosphere that is a testament to its popularity.

"Why do you think people are always rushing? Do they ever stop for a moment and consider how life would be if only they took their time and were in the moment?"

"Yes, you are right, same thing we discussed before to get to the library. Have you ever wondered why some people find it challenging to be alone? It's an intriguing question that makes you think."

Jade savours her coffee's warm, rich flavour as she delicately grasps Simone's hand, their fingers interlacing in a comforting and intimate gesture.

"People tend to avoid being alone with their thoughts and feelings. They seem almost afraid of what they might discover if they truly delve into their inner selves. Instead, they distract themselves with various forms of entertainment, social media, and other activities that keep their minds occupied and focused elsewhere. It's as if they're running away from the essence of who they are, unwilling to confront their fears, desires, and vulnerabilities. Perhaps it's because they believe that they might uncover something they're not ready to face by doing so. Whatever the reason, this tendency to avoid introspection can lead to a sense of disconnection, anxiety, and an overall lack of fulfilment in life." Commented Jade.

"I agree with you" answers Simone.

As they enjoy their conversation, a charming couple crosses their path accompanied by a stunning golden canine. This furry friend boasts a lustrous coat, big, beautiful brown eyes, delightful floppy ears, and a cheerful expression that radiates happiness.

"Simone..."

"Yes?"

"I want one. Look at him...he's so cute."

Looking over, we notice Jade gesturing excitedly towards the cutest little dog she has ever seen!

"One day, maybe." Says Simone, smiling.

Jade's eyes remain fixated as she tracks the movement of the dog.

"Can you imagine us with a dog? Perhaps one of those that wakes us up with their joyful barks and *urges us to take them outside. At first, we may grumble, but then we appreciate the beauty of the early morning sky."*

"Miss Garcia, you make me want things I never thought I needed. Why do you have such power over me? I can't resist your persuasive charm." Says Simone

Jade leans to kiss Simone.

"Should we go?" Jade asks.

Simone rises without a word and gently takes Jade's hand, leading her towards their journey home.

As they stroll along the winding path, the river flowing gently alongside them fills their ears. The soft rustle of leaves and birds chirping provides a soothing background melody. They take a sip of the steaming coffee, relishing the rich aroma and how it warms their hands. They pause momentarily to admire the view, watching the ripples on the water and the birds gliding overhead. As they continue their walk, the coffee fuels them with renewed energy, making the experience all the more enjoyable.

14

"Where will you bring me tonight? Where is it?" Asked Jade.

"No, don't start. I won't tell you until we get there."

"No, I mean, do I have to dress nice?"

Simone bursts into laughter.

"I haven't thought about it, but you could."

Jade smiles for a moment.

"Could I? Please give me a hint or tell me something... you are killing me."

"I love you, Miss Garcia."

The couple still walk along the river, gazing at the clouds above and the trees dancing around them.

The sun sets earlier each day as autumn approaches, making the evenings feel longer. The clock is ticking towards 16:30. the world outside is shrouded in darkness, with only a few streetlights illuminating the sidewalks.

Simone takes Jade's hand by the river and puts it in his pocket to keep her warm from the cold wind.

"Shall we go home now, get changed and go to this mysterious place?" Asked Jade.

"Oh yeah, that was the plan."

"We'll need to call an Uber since it's a 45-minute drive."

"What? Are you bringing me to Australia?"

"I said minutes, not hours." Smiling back to Jade.

The couple strolled towards their humble abode as the sun slowly descended towards the horizon, casting long shadows across the city streets. They walked past the quaint shops and cafes, taking in the sights and sounds of the bustling city. As the last flicker of daylight faded away, the darkness enveloped them in its cool embrace. The couple quickened their pace, eager to reach the warmth and familiarity of their cosy flat. They could see their building in the distance, its brick facade illuminated by the soft glow of the streetlights. As they approached, they noticed the faint scent of freshly baked bread wafting from the nearby bakery. They exchanged a smile, knowing that the day's best moment had yet to come. Finally, they reached the entrance and ascended the stairs.

With a spring in her step, Jade makes her way to her room, eager to change out of her walk clothes. As she begins to undress, a sudden memory jolts her - she had forgotten to mention seeing Tiberius again!

Simone chooses to forgo a change of clothes and retains his current attire, recognising that the attention should be directed towards Jade.

Instead, he chooses to stay seated on the comfortable sofa. He begins scrolling through his inbox, eagerly searching for any potential job offers in acting while waiting for Jade to be ready.

Jade, who was in her bedroom, decided to switch up her wardrobe and experiment with a new style. As she was trying on different outfits, a sudden idea struck her.

"Can we take the bus?" She says out loud.

Simone shuts the laptop with a decisive click, his fingers lingering on the excellent metal surface for a moment before he rises from the plush sofa, his lithe form stretching as she stands.

"Why? It will take longer."

"I will be ready soon. I promise to get out of here fast."

"Okay, let me check the route on the phone."

Simone fumbles and unlocks his phone to check the quickest route to their destination on the map. After comparing the results, he realises that his phone's suggested route will take less time than booking an Uber. He reassures her, *"The bus route is better, my love. It will save us some time, but we must still hurry."*

"Okay, I'm almost done," says Jade loudly from the other room.

Jade makes her way into the living room, her graceful presence drawing Simone's eyes towards her. She wears a breath-taking white dress that clings to her curves in all the right places, accentuating her feminine figure. The dress is perfectly complemented by cream-coloured low heels, which add a touch of sophistication to her overall look. Every detail of her outfit has been carefully thought out, from the delicate lacework on the dress to the subtle shimmer of her shoes.

"Wow!" exclaimed Simone.

"You look stunning."

"Thank you. Shall we go?"

As they take slow, measured steps towards the exit door, the air around them is infused with the rich, floral notes of the perfume Jade had just applied. The fragrance is intense but not overpowering, and it subtly changes character as they move, revealing new layers of complexity with each passing moment. The top notes of bergamot and lemon blend perfectly with the heart of jasmine and rose, while the base notes of vanilla and musk provide a warm, comforting finish. The scent seems to linger in the air long after they have passed, leaving a trail of its captivating aroma in their wake.

"You love the perfume I got for you."

"I love you more than the perfume."

Simone smiles.

"After you, Miss Garcia."

15

With Jade's hand in his, Simone confidently strides ahead, setting the pace for their walk. The rhythm of their steps is in sync, creating a soothing melody as they move forward. The warmth of their intertwined fingers spreads through their bodies, filling them with comfort and security.

They get to the bus station.

The electronic display installed at the bus stop, updated in real-time, indicates that the next bus on this route will arrive in precisely four minutes. The display is programmed to show the bus's estimated arrival time based on its current location and traffic conditions.

"We got here on time. Nice job, Jade."

With a broad smile, he enthusiastically gave Jade a congratulatory high-five and pulled her in for a warm and heartfelt hug.

"Are you ready?" *Simone asks.*

"Whenever I'm faced with a surprise, my body reacts in an instant. My heart rate increases, my palms clammy, and my thoughts jumble. I feel overwhelmed and uncertain as if my mind is rapidly scanning different scenarios and possible reactions to calculate the best course of action."

Jade's eyes darted around anxiously. It was clear that she was feeling nervous about the surprise.

"Despite my best efforts, the fear of making the wrong decision lingers in my mind, making it difficult to fully relax and enjoy the moment."

"I think you are doing very well," Simone assures her.

With its characteristic rumble and hiss, the bus finally arrives at the stop where Simone and Jade are waiting.

They both stand together, their eyes fixed on the approaching vehicle. The stop is deserted except for them, with the empty street stretching out in both directions, silent and still. As the bus comes to a halt, Simone and Jade step forward eagerly, ready to board and start their journey.

"After you, Miss. Your grace and elegance deserve to lead the way."

Simone holds Jade's hand to help her board the bus safely.

"Thank you," Jade replies, smiling.

They scanned the aisle for empty seats as they stepped onto the bus. However, as they made their way towards the back of the bus, they realised that every seat was occupied. The air was thick with the murmur of conversations and the shuffling of feet as they stood awkwardly among the crowd of passengers.

After a walk to the end of the bus, they finally found a couple of empty seats in the middle. However, the seats were not next to each other, and they had to sit apart, as standing was not an option.

"If you would like, I can sit here, and you can sit behind there."

"I'll miss you." Says Jade playfully.

"I can feel the tension building up as I wait for the clock to tick. These forty-five minutes are going to feel like an eternity." Answers Simone smiling

As they lock eyes, a smile spreads across both their faces. With a quick glance around, they each sit in their spot.

Simone and Jade are sitting five seats apart from each other.

Simone eagerly slips on his noise-cancelling headphones and cranks up the volume to its maximum, immersing himself in his favourite tunes' pulsating beats and soaring melodies.

Jade's eyes fixate on him from a distance, observing his every move. She can't help but smile to herself, feeling a warm sensation spreading throughout her body.

Jade is sitting in her seat, with her mind focused on Simone. Suddenly, she feels a palpable sense of unease, as if someone is watching her. Before she can react, a man appears from behind her seat. With a determined gait, he leans closer to her, his features shrouded in shadow.

"It's nice to meet you again."

Jade slowly turns her head to the right and catches sight of Tiberius, who is seated directly behind her.

"You are following me. What's wrong with you?" Says Jade, whispering.

"Again, I can say the same thing about you."

The bus, an ageing vehicle with faded paint and a distinct smell of gasoline, suddenly hits the brakes with a loud screech, causing a jarring jolt that sends passengers lurching forward in their seats. The force of the abrupt stop causes loose items to tumble from overhead compartments and bags to slide off of laps. The driver, a middle-aged man with a stern expression, leans over the steering wheel as if trying to catch his breath. It's unclear what caused the sudden stop, but passengers exchange worried glances, speculating about potential hazards on the road ahead.

Tiberius moves forward to prevent Jade from hitting the front seat.

Jade looks at Tiberius for a second without saying anything.

"You're welcome."

"Is there any other way I can ask you for some privacy? Your understanding and cooperation in this matter would be greatly appreciated." Jade says, trying to be respectful.

Tiberius's countenance seems clouded with melancholy, and his face is marked with a frown.

Jade speaks in hushed tones, careful not to disrupt the surrounding silence. She mainly takes care to avoid drawing the attention of Simone, sitting five seats away, lost in the melody of his music.

"I'm sorry, but I don't believe you deserve forgiveness for what you did," Jade exclaimed.

"What if I can prove you wrong?"

"How would you prove me wrong? Are you going to tell me it was a mistake to enter someone's else vagina?"

Tiberius notices that Jade's temper is starting to flare up. The tension in the air is palpable as Jade becomes increasingly irritable.

"Yeah, well, I wouldn't say that…"

"Then explain, please."

As the bus moves along, the tense atmosphere inside is palpable. Passengers avoid eye contact and focus on their activities, such as reading or listening to music. Yet, it's hard to ignore the tension between two individuals on opposite sides of the aisle. Their voices get louder sometimes, and their body language becomes more aggressive, making the other passengers feel uneasy and on edge. Everyone hopes the situation will be resolved quickly and peacefully so they can continue their journey without further incidents.

Simone sits comfortably in his seat with his eyes closed, fully immersed in the soulful melody of "Mary on a Cross," one of his all-time favourite songs. He feels the music pulsating through his body, filling him with nostalgia and longing. Every note and every beat seem to transport him to a different time and place, weaving a story he can feel in his bones. Despite the world around him being chaotic and unpredictable, this moment of tranquillity and bliss is all he needs to forget his worries and surrender to the beauty of the music.

"What do you want me to explain? The actual moment or what?"

"The 'why' you did that... you stupid."

As Tiberius starts speaking again, Jade quickly stops him talking. She looked up at him with a determined expression and resumed speaking, her words flowing out rapidly as she tried to convey her message as clearly and persuasively as possible.

Jade's heart was beating fast as she spoke with increasing speed, her nerves on edge. She's exasperated and frustrated, her voice trembling as she tries to clarify her point. "Honestly, I don't even care why you did that. I've already asked you once, actually twice. I want you to leave me alone," she says, her words sharp and laced with palpable annoyance.

"I have a boyfriend now, and he's over there."

Jade points in the middle of the bus.

"Does he know you keep meeting me?" Tiberius responds with a malign smile.

When Jade catches wind of Tiberius's words, a sudden wave of hot embarrassment washes over her, causing her cheeks to turn red.

She decides not to answer.

"Why are you travelling separately?"

"It's none of your business Tiberius. It would significantly improve the situation if you were to leave from the bus."

"I get it. Have fun, Jade."

As soon as the bus stops, Tiberius steps forward and carefully places his feet on the pavement before slowly leaving. He takes a deep breath and looks around, taking in his surroundings and the people bustling about as he steps onto the sidewalk.

Jade takes a deep breath and looks at Simone, who is still focused on the song he's listening to with his eyes closed.

Jade turns her head towards the left, her eyes fixated on the brightly illuminated streetlights reflected on the bus's glass window. The yellow glow of the streetlamps casts a warm hue on the passing scenery, creating a serene atmosphere in the otherwise bustling city. The cars whiz past in a blur, leaving behind a trail of red and white lights that seem to dance in the night. Jade takes a deep breath, feeling a sense of relaxation as she watches the world go by.

Simone notices that they are approaching their stop. He turns his head towards Jade and catches her gaze, gesturing with a nod that it's time for them to exit the bus. As the vehicle stops, Simone rises from his seat and waits patiently for Jade to join him before making their way towards the exit.

They finally step off the bus, their bodies buzzing, excited to be reunited after a long separation. As they stop on the sidewalk, Jade turns to Simone and gently takes his head in her hands, pulling him close to her. With a soft smile and a twinkle in her eye, she leans in and presses her lips to his, savouring his warmth and the taste of his mouth on hers. The kiss deepens, becoming more passionate and urgent, as they wrap their arms around each other and lose themselves in the moment.

Simone smiles. "Wow, you still don't know what the surprise is."

Simone catches Jade's gaze, and their eyes lock in an intense connection.

"You have always surprised me in the most delightful ways!"

16

With a gentle smile, Simone reaches out and takes hold of Jade's hand, interlacing his fingers with Jade's. Together, they walk towards a quaint little wooden house with a slanted roof and a charming front porch, surrounded by colourful wildflowers swaying in the gentle breeze. As they approach the house, Simone points out the intricate carvings on the front door, welcoming Jade to their destination with a warm and friendly tone.

"Is this a place where you get to unwind and relax? Looks like a hotel to me!"

"Possibly."

"It doesn't look charming from the outside." Answers Jade, showing a bit of nervousness.

"Please don't judge something based on its appearance. You have taught me this valuable lesson."

"You are right. I'm sorry."

Simone's smile widens as he eagerly anticipates what's to come in just a moment.

Simone takes a deep breath and slowly approaches the old wooden door. He raises his hand and gently knocks on the rough surface, feeling the vibrations in his fingertips. The sound echoes through the empty hallway, making his heart and Jade's race with anticipation. They now wait patiently, listening to the faint creaks and groans of the ancient building, wondering what lies behind the door.

The young couple stands on the porch, shifting their weight from one foot to another as they wait patiently for someone to answer the door. After a few moments, the sound of shuffling feet can be heard on the other side of the door, and soon enough, an elderly woman in her seventies appears, her warm smile welcoming the couple inside.

"Are we going to buy this place?" Jade asks.

"Perhaps, just perhaps, in your dreams." Answer Simone, smiling.

"Nice to meet you, Jade; I'm Anna."

Jade's mind is confused as she tries to comprehend how the unfamiliar woman in front of her knows her name. She searches her memory for any connection or prior encounter, but nothing seems to be coming to mind.

"Simone talked about you and how you love each other; it's like a dream."

"Oh wow... I think so. I don't know what to say." Says Jade timidly.

Jade looks at Simone for a moment and grips his hand more tightly.

"Come on in. Make yourself comfortable. I'm returning in a few seconds."

They are greeted by a charming blend of modern and traditional styles as they enter the ancient house. The archaic walls and intricate woodwork perfectly complement the contemporary furnishings, creating a harmonious and inviting atmosphere. The attention to detail in every corner of the house speaks volumes about the woman's love for both the past and the present, making it a truly unique and captivating space.

Anna gestures towards the sofa, indicating that the couple should take a seat. They sink into the plush cushions, making themselves comfortable. While Anna appears calm and collected, Jade seems to be a bundle of nerves, her excitement mixed with a hint of apprehension.

The sofa is a spacious, inviting piece of furniture with generously cushioned seats that provide a cosy and comfortable seating experience.

"Can you tell me now?"

"Of course not."

Simone turns and smiles at Jade again.

The cosy atmosphere inside the house is made even more inviting by the warmth emanating from a small fireplace next to them, casting a flickering glow across the room. The crackling of the logs and the soft, comforting heat create a sense of tranquillity and comfort, making it the perfect place to relax and unwind.

The woman slowly pushes the door open and steps into the room, her eyes scanning the space as she takes in her surroundings. In one hand, she holds a small, intricately crafted wooden box, which she cradles gently against her chest. As she approaches, her fingers brush lightly over the smooth surface of the lid, which is open to reveal a delicate treasure nestled inside.

As Jade eagerly gazes at the mysterious box before her, her eyes widen with anticipation and apprehension. She can't help but wonder what secrets the box might hold and what its contents could reveal.

"What's in there?" Ask Jade.

As the woman sets down the box, Jade's previously polite expression transforms into a broad, beaming smile that stretches across her face, as if this simple action has brought her immense joy and delight. Her eyes light up with excitement and wonder, as though she's witnessing something truly special and magical. It's a moment that seems to have captured her heart and imagination, and she can't help but revel in the joy and wonder of it all.

A low-pitched and almost indistinct sound resembling a dog's bark can be perceived emanating from the box's interior.

A small Labrador puppy bursts out of the box, playfully displaying its energetic personality. Its soft fur and cute appearance make it irresistible to Jade.

Jade's eyes light up at the tiny puppy walking towards her with hesitant steps. A wide smile spreads across her face, revealing her joy and excitement at the adorable little creature before her.

"Wow, I'm completely blown away. This is beyond anything I ever imagined."

Anna's face lit up as she spoke to the couple, "Caring for him demands a great deal of attention and patience, as he is still finding his way in the world. But his unwavering loyalty and adorable quirks make it all worthwhile. I promise he will bring you endless joy and happiness, especially when you see the world through his curious eyes."

Jade's eyes were filled with tears of exhilaration and overwhelming happiness as she gazed out at the breath-taking dog's figure.

She couldn't believe how lucky she was to be experiencing such a beautiful moment, and the tears that trickled down her cheeks were a testament to the overwhelming joy she felt in her heart.

"He's beautiful." The only words she barely says.

"He's beautiful. Is he for us? Is he ours?" She repeats.

Jade is unsure where to direct her gaze.

She held the dog close to her chest and showered it with kisses.

"He is the last that I'll give away. It is not due to a lack of love or care for him, but rather my age and inability to provide the necessary attention and support he requires. He is a loving and affectionate animal who deserves a warm and welcoming home like the one you can provide."

Jade suddenly turns to Simone.

"When did you...? That is one of the most beautiful surprises anyone could have ever done for me."

"I told you I'm awesome."

The air in the old house is thick with a sense of joy and excitement, creating a positively euphoric atmosphere.

As they observe the scene, they notice the puppy energetically sprinting around the house's interior. Its playful and adorable manner of moving has caught the attention of the three presents, resulting in bouts of laughter echoing throughout the premises.

Simone and Jade spend a few moments playing with the dog, feeling its soft fur and tossing a ball for it to catch. He smiles warmly at Jade before leaving Anna to enjoy her own company.

"Shall we go now? Anna's time is valuable, so I want to ensure every moment counts."

"Yeah, sure, you're right." Answers Jade, rising from the sofa.

Jade's body pivots towards Anna, her arms extending to wrap around Anna in a loving embrace.

"Wow, I'm thrilled that you made it happen! Having a puppy to play with has always been a dream of mine. Thanks a million for making it come true!"

"I can see it." Replies Anna, smiling.

Just as Jade was about to leave the old woman's house, the woman reached out and handed her a creased piece of paper. The paper was yellowed with age and seemed torn out of a book. Jade could see some words scribbled in spidery handwriting on the paper that she couldn't quite make out. She turned to the woman, who had a strange expression, and asked if she could tell her what was on the paper.

"What's that?"

"That's for you to read when you are home and to keep with you."

"Thank you. I will read it once at home then."

"Get back safe".

"Bye-bye," Simone repeatedly says.

17

Simone and Jade step outside, reaching for some fresh air. As they walk out, Jade bends down to scoop up the little dog and cradles it in her arms. The dog yawns and stretches, clearly happy to be with his new family. Simone takes a deep breath of the crisp air and feels the cool breeze brush against his face. Together, they begin to stroll down the path, chatting and giving attention to their new friend.

"It's so lovely to see you smiling all the time," Simone says, looking at Jade.

"Well, this smile is just because of you."

Jade attempts to lower the dog to the ground to test if he can walk on the cold asphalt, but it's evident he's having difficulty.

"When we get home, I have to send a picture to Mom. How are we going to call him?"

"It's your choice. It's yours, babe."

"Can we call him Cutie? To remind my old dog?"

"Yes, anything you want."

Simone's fingers lightly graze Jade's silky hair as he gently leans in to kiss her cheek.

With unwavering determination, Simone abruptly comes to a stop, deftly retrieves his phone, and confidently books an Uber ride without a moment's hesitation.

"I'm going to get us an Uber, babe. It's too cold."

"Yeah, you are right. It got chilled."

"I agree with you! It's gotten colder, hasn't it?"

Simone unlocks his phone and opens the Uber app. He inputs her destination and confirms the ride request. The app shows that the nearest driver is only three minutes away from their location. Simone eagerly awaits the arrival of his ride, looking forward to a comfortable trip back home.

"Only three minutes away, and with no traffic, we'll get home in twenty minutes."

Feeling tired and not in the mood to cook, Simone suggested ordering food. "Shall we order some food? What do you feel like having?" Simone asks.

"How about some delicious sushi?" came the prompt response from Jade, who flashed a smile.

Simone headed inside the car, and as he approached the passenger seat, he reached into his pocket again to grab his phone and open the Deliveroo app. He shows to Jade the option they have. Jade's stomach grumbled as she scrolled and looked through the options, finally settling on a delicious sushi platter. With a few taps, they placed the order and closed the app, ready to satisfy their hunger for the upcoming meal.

Simone and Jade, both beaming with excitement, eagerly carry Cutie in their arms as they enter the front door of their cosy apartment. They carefully set him down on the living room floor, where he takes in his new surroundings with curious eyes and a wagging tail. The space is decorated with tasteful touches of greenery, cosy throw pillows, and a plush rug underfoot. Simone and Jade show Cutie around as they settle in for the evening.

The trio enjoys the sushi together as it arrives almost at the same time they got home, with Cutie happily munching on his new favourite treats.

"Wow, look at that pure joy on his face!" Simone exclaimed.

Jade reached into her pocket and retrieved the crumpled paper the woman had handed her earlier.

"Can I read it out loud?" Asks Jade.

"Yes."

Jade begins to peruse its contents with her eyes fixed on the paper.

"Dear friend,

As I write this letter, tears well up in my eyes. It is with a heavy heart that I bid you farewell. You have been a loyal companion, always offering a wagging tail and a big wet kiss whenever I needed it.

I will never forget how you would greet me at the door after a day outside, tail wagging so hard that your whole body would shake. Or you would snuggle up next to me on the couch, content to be near me.

You have brought so much joy into my life, and I am forever grateful for our time together. I will miss our walks in the park, our games of fetch, and how you would curl up at my feet when I read a book.

But as much as it hurts to say goodbye, I know it is time for you to go. You have brought so much love and happiness into my life, and it is only fair that I let you go with dignity and grace.

So, my dear friend, I know you will always hold a special place in my heart. And though you may be gone, you will never be forgotten.

With love and fond memories,

Anna"

Jade's eyes well up, and tears spilt down her cheeks, leaving glistening trails in their wake.

"She is the cutest person I've ever met," she says, looking at Simone and Cutie.

Feeling overwhelmed by her emotions, Jade slowly extends her arm and gently motions to Simone, silently conveying her desire for a warm and comforting embrace.

Simone stands up from his seat and takes slow steps towards Jade. As he approaches, he reaches out her arms and embraces Jade tightly, holding her in a warm and comforting hug.

"Have you ever had that feeling of seeing someone, and it's like you've met them before? I was looking at her, and she seemed familiar."

"I thought the same right before we left her house, you know?"

"How did you find her?" Ask Jade.

"I searched online for people advertising dogs they were giving away for various reasons. When I called her, she immediately decided she wanted me to go there with you."

"Well, thank you again, babe."

"I must say, it's delightful to see you looking so radiant!"

Simone's gaze was drawn to the clock, the ticking sound filling the silent room. It was then that he realised how late it had become. He stood up from *his chair and approached the bedroom, his footsteps echoing against the hardwood floor. As he entered the room, he noticed the moonlight streaming through the window, casting a soft glow on the bed. Simone sighed, relieved as he was finally ready to settle into the cosy blankets.*

"Do you want him to sleep with us?" Jade asks Simone.

Simone is already in the bedroom, getting undressed.

"Absolutely! That sounds like such a fantastic idea."

Jade turns to Cutie.

"You are the most stunning dog I've ever seen."

With a playful grin, she drops to her knees and showers him with kisses all over his face.

Jade finished getting undressed and took a few minutes to brush her teeth, cleaning each tooth thoroughly. She entered the dimly lit bedroom where Simone was waiting for her, Lying in bed. As

Jade approached, Simone looked up and smiled, his eyes glinting in the soft light.

Jade is on the right side of the bed, Simone on her left and Cutie right in the middle.

"Did you ever dream of having a dog by your side as a kid?"

"Yeah, especially when my grandma passed away."

"Have you ever felt lonely? I know I have. It's a feeling that can sneak up on you when you least expect it." *Simone's heart aches with longing as he reminisces about his grandmother, recalling the warmth of her embrace and the sound of her gentle voice. Memories of their special moments flood his mind, and he yearns for her comforting presence again.*

"I completely understand how you felt. I had a similar experience when my dad walked out on us."

Simone holds Jade's hand.

"Do you miss your grandma?"

"I can't get her out of my head - she's always on my mind."

"Do you ever feel like she's always by your side, no matter where you go?"

"Always," he says, smiling.

The atmosphere in the room suddenly changes, as if a switch has been flipped. The chatter and noise that once filled the space abruptly ceased, leaving an eerie silence. The stillness is palpable, and one can almost hear a pin drop. It's as if time has momentarily stood still, and everyone present is holding their breath, waiting for the next moment to unfold.

They can both hear Cutie's breath.

"I love you." She whispers.

"I love you, too."

18

An unexpected event occurs in the early hours of 6 a.m., deviating from the usual routine. A sharp, high-pitched bark pierced through the silence, echoing off the walls of the dark bedroom. Simone stirred, his eyes slowly opening to the dimly lit room. He could make out the shape of Jade, who was still sleeping soundly beside him. But the barking continued, growing louder and more insistent with each passing moment.

It was their dog, Cutie. The little dog had always been an early riser, but this was different. His barks were urgent, almost frantic as if he was trying to tell them something important. Simone sat up, rubbing the sleep from his eyes, and reached over to turn on the lamp on the bedside table. As the light flooded the room, he saw Cutie staring back at him, his tail wagging furiously, his eyes excitedly bright. It was clear that something was up.

He wanted to go out.

Jade opens her eyes and immediately checks the clock, her gaze lingering on the numbers as she takes in the time.

"Say goodbye to your alarm clock! We have found a new way to wake up in the morning." Simone murmured.

"How convenient," Jade says, stretching her legs and arms.

She then sits on the bed and looks at Cutie, who seems awake for hours and full of energy.

" Thank you for the surprise once again. I think he will bring even more love into the house."

"That's what I wanted to hear."

As Simone slips out of the warm and cosy bedsheets, stretching his limbs and blinking away the remnants of sleep, he feels an incredible rush *of morning air on his skin. He feels the warmth of his soft sheets against his skin. He takes a deep breath and slowly stretches his eyes, adjusting to the lamp light that is making the room less dark. He sits up on the edge of the bed and rubs his eyes again, feeling a sense of tranquillity. He then stands up, feeling the cool air of the room brush against his bare feet as he walks towards the bathroom. He turns on the faucet and allows the water to run until it reaches the perfect temperature. He steps into the shower, feeling the water droplets cascade down his body, washing away any remaining traces of sleepiness.*

Still in bed, Jade snuggles more profoundly into the soft, warm sheets, relishing the comfort of her bed. Cutie wags his tail excitedly, indicating his desire to enter the fresh air. Jade reaches over to pet him, feeling his soft fur beneath her fingertips, before slowly sliding out of bed to begin their day together.

Simone emerged from the shower, water droplets cascading down her glistening skin and forming small puddles on the bathroom tiles.

"I have an upcoming meeting with my agent to discuss my casting."

"The one from yesterday?"

"Yes, about yesterday's audition and what's next."

Jade observes the droplets of water cascading down from Simone's skin.

Jade's sarcasm was palpable as she uttered, "Wow, your ability to create a mess is truly impressive! I'm in awe."

"Sorry."

"It's okay, I was just kidding! Anyway, that sounds nice. When you go downstairs, I will come with you because I'm considering going to the park with Cutie."

"This early?"

"Yeah, I don't mind the dark," answers Jade.

"Okay, babe. Your first date with Cutie. Are you excited?"

"Excited to clean up after him? Absolutely! You can't let a little mess get through a great day."

Jade lay down on her bed's soft, fluffy pillows, feeling content and joyful as a smile crossed her face.

Simone slowly reaches for the curtains, feeling the soft fabric under his fingertips before gently pulling them apart. As he does, a sliver of light peeks through, exposing the darkness outside. The sky is painted in a deep shade of blue, with a smattering of stars twinkling in the distance. The streetlights below illuminate the surroundings, casting a warm glow that fills the room and momentarily blinds him as his eyes adjust to the brightness.

"How is the weather today?" Jade asked.

"Outside looks even clear! But I bet it's pretty chilly out there. Don't forget to bundle up before you head out!"

As they both begin to put on their clothes, Simone experiences a sudden surge of energy, almost like a sudden adrenaline rush. He feels the fabric of his clothes on her skin, taking note of every detail and sensation as the garments slide into place. Getting dressed becomes a moment of heightened awareness and focus as if each article of clothing is imbued with a special significance.

He only has sixty minutes remaining before his scheduled meeting with his agent.

"Are you going to be on time?"

"Yes, I think I also have time for a coffee."

"I will make mine after the walk with Cutie."

Simone and Jade make their way through the heavy wooden door of their apartment building, the sound of it closing behind them echoing through the empty lobby. As they step outside, the *lively sounds of the city engulf them - the honking of cars, the chatter of pedestrians, and the distant hum of music. Cutie snuggles comfortably in Jade's arms, her soft fur brushing against Jade's skin with each step they take. Simone takes a deep breath, feeling the cool breeze on his face, and smiles at Jade, grateful for this moment of peace amidst the chaos of the city.*

He grabs his bicycle from the building's entrance.

The old-style bicycle that Simone is holding has a classic frame design, with a curved top tube and a high seat position. The wheels are smaller than modern bicycles, with a thicker profile with white-walled tires. The handlebars are wide and slightly curved, making them comfortable for long distances. It has a timeless look and feel that is both nostalgic and practical.

"What are you going to do this morning?"

"I am going to the park and try to write a new song when I return. I am feeling very inspired."

Simone leans in and kisses her.

"And maybe I'm going to the coffee shop later," Jade added.

"That's a Good idea. I will come back around 13.00."

"I hope you have a fantastic day, amore."

Simone's lips meet hers in a final farewell before he straddles his trusty bike, anticipating the freedom and thrill of the open road.

The wind whips through his hair, invigorating him with a sense of adventure as he races towards his favourite coffee haunt. The purr of the tires on the pavement provides a comforting backdrop to his thoughts as he looks forward to savouring the robust aroma and smooth taste of his first cup of the day. The traffic is becoming congested, and the streets are filling up with cars and bicycles.

As Simone rides towards his favourite coffee shop, the aroma of freshly brewed coffee fills the air. He can hear the sound of the coffee grinder in the distance, and his mouth waters in anticipation of his favourite beverage's rich, smooth taste. He parks his trusty bicycle outside the shop and leaves it unlocked, knowing the neighbourhood is safe and friendly.

As he entered the coffee shop, many people patiently waiting for their caffeine fix greeted him.

As he hurries to meet with the agent, the man pulls out his phone to check the time. With a sense of urgency driving him forward, he decides to forego his usual stop for coffee and instead focuses on getting to his destination as quickly as possible.

"Damn it. I don't have enough time."

He quickly dashes out of the building onto the bustling street, frantically searching for his bicycle. Finally, he spots it and jumps onto the seat, his heart racing urgently. He deftly weaves in and out of the chaotic traffic, skilfully dodging cars and pedestrians with lightning-fast reflexes, determined to reach his destination as quickly as possible.

19

A commotion in the middle of the road has caught the attention of passers-by. As people draw closer, a crowd forms around a central point. At first, what is happening is unclear, and many assume it might be a heated argument between two men. As the camera pans closer, it becomes apparent that an accident has occurred, and the commotion results from people trying to assist those involved. The scene is chaotic and tense, with bystanders trying to understand what has happened and help in any way they can.

Simone was not wearing a helmet or any other protective gear. His head was completely exposed to the elements, leaving him vulnerable to any unforeseen accidents. The cars and trucks whizzed by him, honking their horns and screeching their brakes as he continued to cycle without a care in the world.

Suddenly, a loud crash occurred, and Simone was thrown off his bicycle. His head hit the pavement hard, and his eyes fluttered as he struggled to stay conscious. With a glance, he spotted his bike just a few meters away. Simone realised he had made a terrible mistake by not wearing a helmet and was now paying the price.

All Simone remembers before the accident is a man driving who hits Simone on his bike and flees.

As Simone lay down on the street, his eyes were drawn to a sleek and stylish black Range Rover that was now driving away.

When the emergency call for assistance was received, a fully equipped ambulance with a team of skilled paramedics was dispatched and reached the scene within minutes. Simone was found lying unconscious on the ground, and the paramedics immediately sprang into action to provide him with the best possible medical care. They assessed his condition, administered vital first aid, and carefully lifted him onto the stretcher to transport him to the hospital for further treatment.

At the same time...

Jade is taking a stroll down a winding path that leads to a small, serene park. The park is surrounded by towering trees that have been around for generations, giving the area a sense of history and permanence. As Jade approaches the park, she hears the sound of dogs barking and playing in the distance. When she arrives, she sees a designated area for dogs to play, complete with obstacles and toys. Cutie, a small and energetic pup, catches her eye as she runs around and barks at other older and bigger dogs. Jade can't help but smile at the sight of such pure joy and enthusiasm.

She stands still, her legs exposed to the sudden gust of icy wind which rushes past her. Her skin pricks with a thousand tiny bumps, and a shiver runs down her spine as the chill penetrates her body. The sensation is intense, and she can almost feel the cold working its way down her bones, leaving her vulnerable and exposed.

"It would help if you stayed close to me."

Cutie starts barking once again. The barking is harmless, typical of small dogs.

Jade's phone suddenly comes to life with a loud, persistent ringing sound demanding her attention.

She then picks up her phone as it vibrates.

"How are you, sweetie?"

Jade just remembered she forgot to call her mom last night about the surprise of her new dog.

"Sorry! I meant to call you last night but got caught up with some stuff. How have you been doing lately? I miss hearing your voice."

"I thought you forgot about me."

"Sorry, Mum, I wanted to video call this morning anyway."

With a tap on her phone screen, Jade initiates a video call by pressing the video chat button.

Jade's mother is now visible on her phone screen.

Jade's fingers were turning numb, and she struggled to keep her hands still due to the chilly weather. The cold air was causing her hands to tremble uncontrollably, making it difficult for her to carry out the phone call.

"Look what Simone got for us yesterday."

With a determined focus, she raises the camera and directs it straight at Cutie, now clearly visible on the bustling sidewalk — the camera lens zooms in, capturing every detail of Cutie's appearance and surroundings.

"Oh my god, who's that?"

"Simone had planned this a few weeks ago. It's almost like fate, considering you called me yesterday about Cutie dying."

"He is so cute. How old is he?"

Jade's eyes light up with joy as she looks down at the tiny creature in her arms. A comprehensive, infectious grin spreads across her face and refuses to disappear. "He's only three months old," she exclaims, her voice filled with tenderness and affection. "His name is Cutie."

Jade's mum is in tears as she reminisces about the recent loss of her dog.

As Jade focuses intently on the video call, her phone repeatedly vibrates, plastering her screen with a flurry of missed call notifications. Her device's incessant buzzing and flashing are a constant distraction, hindering her ability to engage in the conversation at hand fully. Despite her best efforts to ignore the interruptions, the persistent alerts continue to demand her attention, creating a sense of urgency that cannot be ignored. "Mom, can I call you later? Someone is contacting me, but it's with an unknown number."

"Sure, I'll take some rest now. You can give me a call tomorrow."

"I love you, mom."

"I Love you," Maria says.

Jade hangs up the video call and answers straight to the constant call she's getting.

"Hello?"

"Hello, Miss Garcia?"

Jade could sense the caller's anxiety and tension even before they spoke. The words that followed were rushed and breathless as if the caller was struggling to convey an urgent message. The tone was infused with worry and concern, and Jade could feel the urgency in their voice as they spoke. With a sense of foreboding, she answered.

"Yes, who's speaking?" The reply came solemnly, "Hello, this is the hospital department. We regret to inform you that Simone has been involved in an incident."

Jade's heart skipped a beat, and she felt a sudden chill run down her spine as the doctor's words echoed in her mind. She stood frozen in place, unable to move or speak, as her thoughts raced with fear and uncertainty. The room seemed to spin around her, blurring the figures of the medical staff and the medical equipment. Every sound seemed amplified, making her feel even more vulnerable and exposed.

"What? How? When?"

Jade kneels and holds Cutie close to her.

"Can I ask you if you can come to the Academics Medics Centrum?"

"Sure, I'll be there any time from now."

As Jade ends the phone call, her heart races, anticipating the task. She takes a deep breath and steps out onto the bustling street, her eyes scanning for any sign of an available taxi. The honking of cars, the chatter of people, and the sound of music from nearby shops merge into a cacophony of noise around her. She weaves through the crowd, dodging pedestrians and street vendors, her gaze fixed on the road ahead. She tries to flag down every taxi, but they are all occupied. Despite the frustration, she keeps moving forward, determined to reach her destination on time.

After several attempts to hail a taxi, she finally catches the attention of a taxi driver, who stops his car for her. She opens the door and steps inside, Cutie in her hands, grateful for the refuge from the bustling street. The scent of air freshener and leather seats surrounds her, creating a sense of comfort and security as the driver asks where to go.

Jade quickly gets into the taxi and tells the driver where to go.

"To the Academics Medics Centrum. It's an emergency."

"I'll try to go as fast as possible."

Without wasting time, the driver firmly presses his foot on the accelerator pedal, causing the car to speed up and zoom swiftly towards the hospital. He focuses all his attention on the road ahead, determined to get there as quickly as possible. Knowing that every second counts, he doesn't ask further questions or waste time on unnecessary conversations. The situation's urgency is palpable as the car dodges through traffic, expertly manoeuvring around obstacles and making sharp turns. The driver's eyes are fixed firmly on the road ahead as he navigates through the busy streets precisely, his sole goal being to get to the hospital as fast as possible.

Jade suddenly feels a wave of numbness wash over her, and a flood of negative thoughts consumes her mind.

After a couple of minutes, they reach their destination.

With nervousness and impatience, Jade hastily opens the taxi door and exits the pavement. Despite the slight jolt of the taxi as it comes to a stop, Jade's tight grip on Cutie never wavers as she carefully makes her way out. Her eyes light up with joy as she finally sets foot outside, eager to run into the hospital.

As she exits the car, she drops a wad of cash into the driver's hand without acknowledging him. The amount is far more than required for the trip. The driver mutters a polite "Thank you" and a "Good luck" as she walks away, but he knows she won't even hear his words.

Jade enters the hospital with a nervous look and frantically inquires about Simone's whereabouts. Her heart racing, she darts from one staff member to another, hoping to find the answers she desperately seeks.

"Are you Simone's girlfriend?"

The lead physician approaches the reception desk. He greets Jade as she inquires about Simone's condition, asking detailed questions to understand the situation better.

"Yes, Someone called me about an incident but didn't provide any details."

"Yes, I called you."

Jade now recognises the doctor's voice.

"How is he? What happened to him?"

"A car ran over him in the traffic. He's now conscious, which is good, but someone is in the room with him as he rests."

"Who's with him now? Can I see him?"

"Yeah, you can follow me."

20

As she steps inside the hospital's corridor, Jade's eyes are greeted by a bright, luminous atmosphere filling the room. The walls are painted in a soothing shade of white, and the ceiling is adorned with rows of fluorescent lights that create an even distribution of light. The illumination is so intense that it penetrates every corner of the room, casting a warm, inviting, comforting, and reassuring glow. The brightness of the interior is a testament to the hospital's commitment to creating an environment conducive to healing and recovery.

Jade walks behind the doctor, briskly leading her towards Simone's room. The hallway is quiet except for their footsteps echoing against the walls.

As Jade enters the dimly lit room, her eyes meet Lucian's piercing gaze for the first time. The air is thick with tension, and she can feel her heart racing in her chest as she takes in his chiselled jawline and intense stare.

Lucian turns around and greets Jade.

"Hi, I'm Lucian, Simone's best friend.

"I'm Jade, his girlfriend."

"I know. He talked about you without any breaks yesterday."

A brief smile crosses Jade's face.

"How is he?"

As she takes a deep breath, she's greeted by the undeniable scent of disinfectants and antiseptics infused with the subtle hum of hospital machinery. The smell is potent yet refreshing, filling the air in the room with an unmistakable crisp and clean aroma. The disinfectants used to keep the hospital environment sterile can be easily detected, but they are not overpowering. The hum of the machines acts as a gentle backdrop, providing a sense of comfort and security amidst the clinical setting. The coolness of the temperature-controlled environment provides a sense of calm and comfort, making it a perfect spot for rest and recovery.

"Lucky...Did you know he was riding the bike without a helmet?" asked Lucian.

"I told him many times to use it."

When Jade encounters Lucian, a wave of comfort and tranquillity washes over her. The mere presence of Lucian seems to have a calming effect on Jade, making her feel at ease and more relaxed.

As Simon lies in bed, he looks peaceful and relaxed, with only a few minor injuries visible on his face. There are bruises around his forehead, and a small cut can be seen on his lip. Despite these injuries, he seems to be recovering well and showing no discomfort.

Jade walks closer to Simone while still talking to Lucian.

"Have they figured out how it all went down? And do they have any leads who might have been behind the wheel?"

"All I was interested in was his state. If he was okay or not. He is currently sleeping, but according to them, he is very healthy."

Jade slowly closes the gap between herself and Simone, her eyes locked onto his hair. As she approaches, she reaches out his hand, her fingers uncurling to trace Simone's hair strands. Her touch is soft and delicate as if she's afraid to disturb the perfect arrangement of each hair on his head. Simone's hair is thick and lush, and she can feel the *weight of it in her hand as she runs her fingers through it. The sensation is soothing, and she finds herself lost in the moment, captivated by the softness of his hair.*

The immense relief I feel knowing that the situation is not severe is indescribable.

"You have no idea how grateful I am that it's nothing severe."

"Yeah, same."

Lucian's gaze abruptly shifted towards the clock on the opposite wall, and a feeling of dread washed over him as he noticed that he was already behind schedule for his training session. His heart sank as he realised he had to rush to make it on time.

"I have to go training now but will get back right after. Are you going to be here?"

"Yes. I want to be here when he awakes."

He quickly bends down to pet Cutie.

"Okay. Nice to meet you again, and I'll see you later."

He could feel the weight of disappointment settling in as he hurriedly gathered his things and rushed out the door.

At the same time...

Jade settles into a plush armchair beside Simone's bed, her unwavering gaze fixated on Simone, her expression a blend of worry and care.

She's looking at Simone and reaches out to hold his hand, but as her fingers wrap around his, she feels a sudden chill. Alarmed, she quickly checks his pulse and notices that his hand feels cold. Without wasting a moment, she immediately calls for a doctor, hoping they can provide answers and help.

"Doctor? Anyone?" Jade shouts.

Suddenly, a doctor burst into the room with a look of worry etched on his face, as if something urgent had happened.

"What's the problem?"

"Why his hands are extremely cold?"

"Oh, it's okay. If you have cold hands, it might indicate that your body is trying to regulate its temperature. He's resting and okay."

"Sorry, I didn't mean to cause anything."

The doctor reassures Jade with a gentle smile and makes his way towards the door, his lab coat swishing softly behind him.

As she gazes out of the window, she notices a sliver of sunlight piercing through the glass, illuminating the room and casting a warm and inviting aura that envelops the space. The soft rays of light paint the walls with a golden hue, creating a soothing and comforting atmosphere that instantly lifts my mood. The room once shrouded in darkness, now brims with life and vitality, thanks to this gentle yet powerful interplay of light and shadow.

As the clock ticks by, an entire hour slips away, and Jade feels more at ease. She takes out her phone and jot down some notes, her fingers moving quickly across the screen.

Cutie is next to her resting, too.

Her fingers are tapping away at the screen of her smartphone as she intently focuses on crafting a new melody. With a music composition app open on her device, she is experimenting with various notes and rhythms to perfectly capture the emotions she wishes to convey through her music.

Jade puts her headphones on so as not to make any noise.

As the door slowly creaks open, a tall figure enters the room. The doctor is dressed in a pristine white coat with a stethoscope draped around their neck, giving off a sense of expertise and authority. Their *face is composed and unwavering, radiating confidence and professionalism.*

"Miss Garcia?"

Despite the doctor's clear presence, Jade is entirely unaware, lost in her own world. She has plugged in her earphones and turned up the volume to the point of blocking out all external noise.

Jade is focused on the music app in the hospital room, her eyes fixed on the screen as the doctor approaches her. As he draws near, she can feel the warmth emanating from his body, and she senses a gentle calmness in his demeanour. The doctor's hand extends towards her, his fingertips making contact with the soft fabric of her shirt before finally coming to rest on her shoulder. She feels the weight of his hand, but it is a reassuring pressure, a reminder that she is not alone in this moment.

"Miss Garcia," he repeats.

"Oh my god, sorry... yes?"

"Just wanted to let you know that there's someone downstairs looking for you. Sounds like it might be important!"

"Now?"

"Yes, right now."

"Can I leave the dog here?" Jade asks.

The doctor looked down from his clipboard and met Jade's gaze before nodding. The doctor understood Jade's concern but knew this hospital had a strict policy against allowing animals. He gently suggested, "It would be better if you had him with you."

"I'm sorry for not knowing that earlier. Anyway, I'm heading downstairs now."

Jade's heart raced as she hastened, her mind consumed with thoughts of who might be approaching her from behind. Every footfall seemed to echo in the silence, raising her anxiety even higher. She couldn't help but wonder if danger lurked in the shadows, ready to pounce at any moment.

She walks through a couple of doors until she gets to the main one and walks through it.

She steps outside with her dog cradled in her arms, and we see the dark-haired figure again.

Jade is giving the guy a rude look.

"What are you doing here? How do you even know I was here?"

Jade's eyes are immediately drawn to Tiberius as he approaches, his long black coat billowing behind him. A mystery surrounds him, and his piercing gaze only adds to the intrigue.

"As soon as I saw the incident unfolding before my eyes, I didn't waste a second to call for an ambulance and get help on its way. Then I realised it was your boyfriend."

"You don't even know him. Have you seen him before?"

Tiberius smiles. However, the smile is quite grim.

"Yesterday, you pointed him at me on the bus? Remember?"

Jade softened up.

"You are right, sorry."

A hush falls between them, filling the space with a palpable stillness.

The two are positioned several meters away, standing still stationary.

Feeling the tension, Tiberius takes it upon himself to initiate a conversation to ease the awkwardness.

The gentle caress of the cool breeze is sending shivers down their spines.

"I remember you mentioning that you've always wanted one."

Says Tiberius, pointing at Cutie.

Jade's smile softens again.

"Yes, Simone gave me a surprise last night."

"You seem happy with him."

"I'm very happy. You have no idea of how special that guy is."

"And how lucky he is."

As Tiberius continues to speak, Jade feels a knot form in her stomach, and her emotions begin to rise, threatening to spill over into tears.

"Could you explain why you think he's lucky?" Asks Jade, appearing more angry.

After Tiberius expressed his gratitude for Simone's survival, he noticed a look of distress on Jade's face. He quickly realised that his initial statement had caused Jade to shift her mood or perhaps come to a realisation. To ease the tension, Tiberius searched for a new way to phrase his words.

"I meant to have found you."

Jade goes back to talking about their past relationship.

"Well, you had your opportunity, Tiberius. We have been together for Seven years. And after being together for seven years, you managed to ruin everything."

The feeling of relaxation and calm that had gradually settled in is suddenly shattered as a surge of anxiousness and tension engulfs the atmosphere, creating a palpable sense of discomfort and uneasiness.

"Can we not make a scene right outside the hospital? Can we go behind there for a moment?"

Tiberius says, pointing behind his car

"Let's talk and settle this once and for all."

21

As they approach the parking lot, Tiberius's sleek black Range Rover comes into view, its polished exterior gleaming under the streetlights. They both make their way towards the intimidatingly large vehicle, with its tinted windows and imposing presence.

The bustling parking lot teems with many cars and bicycles of various makes, models, colours, and sizes. The air is punctuated with the soft hum of engines and the occasional ring of bicycle bells as people move about, each with their own purpose and destination. The scene is a vibrant representation of the hustle and bustle of modern life, with the vehicles serving as symbols of freedom and responsibility and the people moving among them as the embodiment of the perpetual motion of society.

Tiberius looks at Jade with a curious expression and asks, "Can you tell me how you've been feeling over the last seven years?"

Jade takes a deep breath before responding. She thinks back to all the moments she shared with Tiberius - the laughter, the tears, the fights, the makeup. She can feel her heart racing as she replies, "What kind of question is that? I've felt a lot of things. I've felt happiness, sadness, anger, love, and everything else. You were my first everything - my first boyfriend, my first time living with someone, my first love. I loved every moment we spent together, even the tough ones."

It now appears that Tiberius has begun to exert his influence in a way that seems to sway the situation in his favour, possibly through manipulation.

"Why are you asking me to take responsibility for the mistake if you are unwilling to acknowledge the past seven years?"

"So now the problem is me."

"I didn't say that."

"You meant it."

Tiberius's footsteps echo as he approaches Jade; her heart is now pounding with anticipation. As he walks nearer, he can see the delicate features of her face and the way her eyes sparkled in the light.

"I want you to remember our fantastic time together without getting caught up in the small details."

"Small detail? Do you think it's a small detail? Do you think it was nothing?"

"I'm not saying that. I'm just saying I'm very sorry for what happened... it was a moment of weakness."

With a determined gait, Jade strides towards the car and places her weight against it, her arms still holding Cutie, who's remaining silent and calm. The metallic surface of the car is cool to the touch, sending a refreshing shiver down her spine. She takes a deep breath, contemplating her next move.

"Do you want to know the worst of all of this?"

"What is it?" Asks Tiberius.

"You didn't tell me anything. I had to figure it out independently when I noticed your attitude had completely changed." Jade addresses Tiberius

firmly and looks directly into his eyes while speaking.

"I was going to tell you...I didn't know how..."

As Tiberius confidently strides towards Jade, she remains casually leaning against the car. The distance between them slowly diminishes, causing a subtle shift in the atmosphere around them. A hint of a smile tugs at the corners of his mouth while Jade's eyes sparkle with curiosity. The air around them buzzes with unspoken tension, making it clear that something significant will happen.

"Do you remember when you told me that even if something similar happened, we would find the courage to forgive each other?"

"It was one of those moments where my expectations were utterly shattered in the best way possible."

Tiberius gently runs his fingers through the soft fur of Cutie, which wags its tail in contentment.

"Look at me, Jade."

"I can't."

"Yes, you can." Insisted Tiberius

"Then, I don't want to."

The persistence of Tiberius is growing more potent and palpable, making it increasingly apparent.

"Jade, Look at me for a second".

At the same time...

Lucian, who had just completed his early morning training, drives his beautiful sports Nissan into the hospital parking lot. He quickly scans the area for a suitable spot, manoeuvring through the congested lot as he looks for open spaces. After a few minutes of searching, he spots an available parking spot near the hospital entrance. He carefully backs into the spot, ensuring not to hit the cars on either side. Satisfied with his parking job, he turns off the *engine and takes a moment to collect his thoughts before stepping out of the vehicle. He grabs his bag, moves it from the passenger seat to the back seat, and makes his way towards the hospital doors, mentally preparing to greet Simone.*

As he gazes into the distance, he focuses on two silhouettes - a man and a woman - locked in a passionate embrace. they are sharing a tender kiss.

The tension in the atmosphere around Lucian seems to increase as he catches a glimpse of something he was not meant to see. The air becomes thick with an unspoken sense of unease, and it is clear that whatever Lucian witnessed has caused a significant shift in the situation's dynamics.

22

Tiberius moves closer to Jade, places his hand on her waist, and pulls her towards him. He looks into her eyes and leans in slowly, giving her time to pull away if she wants to. But she doesn't. And so, he presses his lips gently against hers, feeling their warmth and softness. However, as soon as he realises it was without her permission, he quickly pulls away, feeling ashamed and guilty.

Jade remains motionless, her expression unreadable. Meanwhile, Lucian's sharp senses pick up on every detail and wastes no time sprinting towards the interior.

With an intense glare in her eyes, Jade wrapped one arm around the furry body of Cutie, securing it tightly against her chest. She then extends her other arm, pushing Tiberius away with a determined force as if repelling an intruder. The dog squirms in her arms, sensing the tension in the parking lot.

"Please stop, Tiberius. My boyfriend is in the hospital, and I love and respect him." Tiberius is urged to halt his actions by Jade, who pleads with him to stop.

"Then why don't you go inside and forget about us?" Asks Tiberius

"I'm trying to do so, but you keep popping up every moment of the day." Exclaimed Jade, shouting out loud.

The heavy white door creaks as Lucian pushes it open, and he steps into the room, his footsteps echoing off the stone walls. The air is thick with the smell of dampness and neglect. Lucian takes a moment to let his eyes adjust to the dim light, and as they do, they settle on Simone, who is lying on a narrow cot. His chest rises and falls in a steady rhythm, and Lucian can see the relief on his face as he registers his presence. He approaches him slowly, taking in every detail of his appearance. His hair is matted and tangled, and his skin is pale and clammy. Despite his weakness, his eyes shine with fierce determination, and Lucian can sense the strength of his will.

"Hey, Lucian. What are you doing here?"

"Hey, I was here before. I went for my training and came back."

"Oh really? Sorry, I don't remember anything after the ambulance picked me up."

"Hey, it's okay." Reassures Lucian

He then takes a short pause.

"How do you feel?"

"You know what? I'm feeling pretty darn good right now!"

"Yeah, the doctors said you are very healthy."

"This is something you already knew." Answers Simone, smiling.

"Yeah, you are correct."

Lucian takes a moment to gather his thoughts before resuming with renewed vigour.

"I met your girlfriend."

Simone smiles at Lucian's words.

"She was here?"

"Yeah."

Suddenly, Lucian's face took on a completely different expression!

"She's cute. Right?"

"Actually..."

Lucian is struggling to find the right words to convey his thoughts.

"You won't believe what I just saw! I was returning from training, and I'm sure I saw her..."

"Where? Is she here?"

"Wait...I think I saw her kissing somebody..."

With a sudden burst of energy, Simone leaps up from the hospital bed, eyes wide with surprise and determination. His hands grip the edge of the mattress tightly as he's trying to stand.

"No, it's not her then... it's impossible."

Lucian observed in the distance for a moment.

"She had a puppy dog with her." Turning back his gaze to Simone

Simone's eyes begin to well up with tears.

"What? Who was she with?"

"I don't know... I saw a tall, dark-haired guy."

"Oh...I don't know anyone...Are you sure?"

With her head held high, Jade glides away from Tiberius, her steps measured and determined, leaving him dejected.

Then she turns once again.

"And please don't follow me anymore. If you continue to do so, I may have to involve the authorities."

Tiberius, feeling defeated, enters the car and retreats into its comfortable embrace. His disappointment hangs heavily upon him as he resigns himself to his current situation.

Jade's footsteps echo down the sterile, fluorescent-lit corridors of the hospital as she retraces her steps to Simone's room. Memories of the winding path flood her mind, the scent of disinfectant and the sound of beeping machines filling her senses.

She is petting Cutie, who is still in her arms.

As she enters the final door, she comes face-to-face with Lucian, who is on his way out.

"Hey Lucian, you are back; you okay?"

As Lucian's words fall on deaf ears, frustration sets in, and his anxiousness manifests in rapid footsteps. He hurries towards the main entrance door, each step echoing through the empty hallway. The sound of his shoes hitting the ground reverberates as he places one foot in front of the other, propelled by a sense of urgency.

Jade walks into the dimly lit room and immediately notices Simone on the bed, his eyes open and glistening with tears. The sight of Simone's wet eyes and the palpable heaviness in the air causes Jade to feel a sense of confusion and concern about Lucian's attitude towards Simone.

"Hey, amore, how do you feel?" Asks Jade.

Jade gets close to Simone and puts her hand around his cheeks.

"Why are you here?" Asks Simone with a different expected attitude.

"What happened? I was called here a few hours ago for an incident, but you were resting."

"And so you decided to go downstairs and kiss someone else."

"What are you talking about?"

"Please don't lie to me. You know what I think about lies."

"How do you know what happened downstairs?"

Simone slowly turns his head, shifting his gaze towards the window on the opposite side of the room. The light filtering through the glass casts a warm glow onto his face, illuminating his features' subtle lines and contours.

"Lucian was coming upstairs when he saw you kissing a guy."

Jade can hear the tension in Simone's voice.

"No, no, no..."

Jade is becoming increasingly agitated.

"I never wanted to kiss him, but he was so insistent. He leaned in, and before I knew it, his lips were on mine. I quickly pushed him away, feeling anger and disgust."

"So it's true... who's this guy?"

"I was going to tell you, but I thought I had gotten rid of my ex-boyfriend alone."

Simone's eyebrows furrow, and his gaze becomes unfocused, displaying a clear sense of bewilderment and uncertainty.

"What was he doing here? Was he in the hospital?"

"He said he was the one who called the ambulance when he saw the incident."

Simone attempted to sit up.

"No, that moment is still so vivid in my memory. It was an old lady who made the call for the ambulance."

Jade now looks confused.

"I was talking to him, and he mentioned that he did it!"

Well, he lied then... do you have a picture of him or something? I still remember what happened... I think I fell unconscious just a few moments later."

"I've blocked him from every platform, but I can find some pictures."

Simone is waiting impatiently.

Jade retrieves her phone from her pocket, unlocks it with a tap of her finger, and searches through her photos until she finds the one she wants. Once located, she holds up her phone to Simone, who peers over to see the image on the screen.

Simone leans in closer, his eyes tracing every contour of the guy in the picture. He studies his expression, how his hair falls across his forehead and his jaw set. Suddenly, excitement rushes through his body, and he jumps up, nearly losing his balance and falling off the bed.

"That is the guy who was behind the wheel! I saw his face, exactly like his." Says Simone loudly.

Jade suddenly is hit by goosebumps all over her body.

"What? How do you know?"

"Tell me. Does he drive a black Range Rover?"

Jade's memory takes her back to the moment she was leaning on the car just a few minutes before. She vividly recalls the car's details; it was the Range Rover they had purchased for Tiberius two years ago, a sleek and stylish vehicle that had always impressed her. The memory brings a sense of sadness to her face.

As Jade gazed ahead, her eyes started well up with tears.

Simone feels Jade's innocence.

"What did he tell you?"

"He told me he saved you and had a moment of weakness when he cheated on me."

"Do you believe him? After all that, you still believed him?"

Jade carefully lifts Cutie, holding the fluffy feline close to her chest as she walks to the plush, comfortable bed. She gently places Cutie onto the soft, cosy surface, ensuring the dog is relaxed, before turning her attention to Simone. Jade takes a step closer, her eyes locked onto Simone's, feeling her heart race with anticipation.

"I didn't know his plan. He followed me everywhere yesterday. However, I thought I had successfully ended any communication with him after I explained that I was committed to you."

"Jade, why didn't you tell me? "

"I know, but you know how we both hate dramas, and I genuinely thought it was all fixed."

Jade gingerly grasps Simone's hands, which retain a frigid chill upon contact.

"You have very cold hands, by the way."

Simone ignores Jade's comment for a moment.

"What about the kiss, Jade?"

Jade directed her gaze to Simone's eyes again.

"I swear, I'm telling you the truth. I quickly pushed him away when he attempted to kiss me."

"Why?"

"What do you mean why? Because I'm with you, and I love you."

Simone became more receptive when she saw the genuineness in Jade's eyes.

"Please, can you trust me?"

"Did he say anything after you pushed him away?"

"I warned him I would involve the police if he approached me again.

"Do you think he will listen to you this time?"

Jade gazes at Simone with a newfound intensity, her eyes fixated on every detail of Simone's face and body language.

"Okay. Let's make a deal. I'll let you deal with him if he comes near me again. Okay?"

Simone's once-uneasy and stressed vocal pitch has undergone a noticeable transformation, as it now emanates a serene, soothing, and comforting quality.

"I like the sound of that."

Jade goes down to kiss Simone.

23

Simone's doctor enters the room to perform a thorough check-up and ensure that her current state of health is stable and satisfactory.

"It seems you've been fortunate, Simone. But you must use protection to keep riding a bike."

"You are right. I'm sorry."

The doctor reassures Simone.

"Don't worry, there's no need to apologise to me. Your girlfriend here got more scared than we did."

Simone gazes in the direction of Jade, studying her intently.

"Now you're good to go. It seems the painkillers worked."

"Can I go home already?"

"You can count on me to take great care of you!" Jade intercepts Simone's answer to the doctor.

"Just make sure he's having a rest day for today." Simone's doctor tells Jade.

"I will." Simone intervenes.

Suddenly, Simone steps in front of everyone in the room, halting their movements and capturing their attention.

Simone holds the dog as he and Jade walk down the corridor together.

"Shall we get an Uber? Or do you prefer to walk?"

"I want to walk a little. I need a coffee, too."

As an avid coffee drinker, Simone suddenly becomes aware that he hasn't yet had his usual morning cup of coffee. He can almost feel the caffeine withdrawal symptoms starting to set in.

"You didn't go to the coffee shop this morning?"

"No... it was hectic, and I couldn't wait any longer because I had to meet my agent."

Panic sets in as he frantically searches every nook and cranny, scanning the corridor with his eyes as he tries to locate his phone. His heart sinks as he realises the device is not in its pocket, and he recalls where he might have left it. The search proves fruitless despite his efforts, leaving him helpless and frustrated.

"Uh-oh, it looks like I've lost my phone. Can you help me find it? I need to call her somehow."

"Don't worry about that; we will do it when we are home." Jade tries to calm Simone down.

"But I don't have it with me."

"Yeah, I heard. We are going to find a way."

Jade can sense that Simone is still feeling stressed from the recent experience they just went through together. The weight of the situation seems to be still lingering in Simone's emotions.

"Cutie's first date turned out to be a complete tragedy."

"He's been excellent and quiet all the time. I wish to have the same attitude towards things."

As they leave the hospital, the timid sun shyly peeks out from behind the clouds, casting its warm glow on their faces. The wind, a bit stronger than before, tousles their hair and clothes.

As they leave the hospital, the couple sets off on foot, following the winding path parallel to the tranquil river, with the sun setting in the distance.

"Sorry, I need to slow down..." says Jade, realising she's walking a bit faster than Simone.

"I'm okay, babe...I can't wait to take a hot shower."

"Do you still want to have a coffee first?"

"Yes, I need one."

After a few minutes of walking, Simone points to the cafe they visited the first time the day before and asks Jade if they can go there.

"Can we go in there?"

They both walked into the coffee shop.

The coffee shop is quiet, with only a few scattered customers sipping their drinks. The faint sound of the coffee machine and soft background music fill the space.

Simone's senses tingle as he senses a pair of eyes fixated on him, sending shivers down his spine.

Right before them, Simone and Jade meet the same old woman they met the day before in the same bar.

"This is the third time I have met you...too many times, Mister."

"Why third time?" Asks Simone.

"I thought I met you yesterday for the first time."

Simone looks at Jade for a second.

"Also this morning..." Add the Old lady.

Jade comprehended and retained this information without delay, remembering Simone's words about an old woman calling for help right after the incident.

"Did YOU call the ambulance this morning?"

The old lady looks at Simone, smiling.

Simone is in complete disbelief!

"Oh my god. I'm grateful."

"I know you are. Yesterday, you helped me; today, I helped you."

"We are grateful." Repeats Jade

"I informed the police about the car that fled the scene. They are on it."

Simone catches Jade's gaze, but this time, there's no smile on her face.

"I'm sure they won't let him get away with it." Says Simone.

The old woman's weathered face softened into a small smile as their eyes met briefly. She reached out her hand to grasp the steaming cup of coffee prepared for her and slowly made her way towards the exit, her footsteps shuffling softly against the tiled floor.

Just before the elderly woman reaches the door, Simone captures her attention again.

"Before you leave, I'm curious to know your name. May I ask for it?"

"Don't you worry, we'll meet again." Says smiling.

"Cute puppy"

Simone and Jade look at each other in disbelief. Their mouths drop open as they process the unexpected turn of events.

"I didn't expect that." Said Simone.

"I know, me neither. Let's get you a coffee," Jade says.

"Do you want one?" Asks Simone back.

"No thanks, I'm already very agitated without it."

They both walked to the counter where Simone placed his order:

"Can I please have an oat latte?"

"Sure," the barista replies.

Jade can hardly believe her eyes as she exclaims, "Today is just too weird! Everything seems to be happening all at once!"

"You are right." Replies Simone, waiting for his coffee to get ready.

"Have a fantastic afternoon, guys!" says the barista.

As they leave the coffee shop, Simone's hands are warmed by the toasty cups of coffee he just purchased. The rich aroma of freshly brewed coffee fills the air as they start making their way back home. They walk side by side, this time in silence and enjoying the peaceful surroundings. The sun shines brightly, casting a warm glow on everything around them, and a gentle breeze carries the sweet scent of blooming flowers. As they approach their neighbourhood, they wave to their neighbour who's out walking their dog and continue towards their home, feeling content and grateful for the simple pleasures in life.

Cutie in Jade's arms is half asleep.

As they approach their home, the clock strikes 17:00, and a sense of hunger and weariness envelops them like a sunny haze.

They purposely took the long route to spend some time in an open space. Simone keeps talking about wanting to get into the shower because he smells like a hospital.

"I can smell it on my skin."

"Okay, grumpy... we are getting home now." Says Jade, smiling.

"I'm not grumpy. I want to take a shower."

"I can take it with you." Answer Jade playfully.

"Oh, that sounds like a nice invitation."

"Does your lips hurt?"

"A little bit, but it's okay...Don't worry about that one bit! It's the least of my concerns."

The sun is slowly dipping below the horizon, painting the sky with a beautiful array of warm colours, while a chilly breeze begins to pick up, leaving a noticeable drop in temperature in the air.

With a sigh of relief, Simone crosses the threshold of the flat, his footsteps echoing against the hardwood floor. He wastes no time as he sets his sights on the bedroom, his mind already racing through the list of tasks he needs to complete before finally allowing himself to relax. He deftly removes his shoes and heads towards the closet, carefully selecting a comfortable set of clothes to change into after the shower. He makes his way towards the bathroom, eager to escape the grime and sweat of the day with a refreshing shower.

"I can make the meal I wanted to prepare for us. I bet you are starving." Says out loud Jade.

"I need to take a shower. Give me a moment."

"Grumpy," she whispers, smiling on her own.

As Simone enjoys a refreshing shower, Jade begins to gather all the necessary ingredients for the delicious vegan meal she had promised to prepare for Simone the day before. She carefully selects each item and organises them neat and orderly, ready to begin cooking.

24

As Jade starts the dish, she carefully adjusts the oven temperature to the exact degree required for optimal cooking. She then selects a suitable pan and places it on the stove to begin warming up. With a watchful eye, she ensures the pan is heated to the ideal temperature before adding the remaining ingredients. Through meticulous preparation, Jade sets the stage for a flavourful and satisfying meal Simone will never forget.

She slices the soft, green potatoes into thin, even rounds with deft hands. Next, she turns her attention to the onions, skilfully dicing them into small pieces before tossing them into the pan. The earthy aroma of mushrooms fills the kitchen as she slices them into thick slices and adds them to the sizzling vegetables. As the ingredients begin to brown and caramelise, she reaches for a selection of spices, carefully measuring the perfect amount to add bold flavour to her dish.

After a long, hot shower, Simone wraps himself in a fluffy towel and enters the kitchen. The streetlights are just starting to peek through the windows, casting a soft glow over the room. The scent of the dinner Jade is preparing tingles. Simone's nose sets about to have his dinner. Simone can't help but smile at their eagerness, appreciating the company of Jade and Cutie.

"You are going to love this."

"I remind you where I'm coming from...Italians don't lie about food." Replies Simone.

"I know. That's why I chose the best thing to do. And to show you how much I love you."

Simone moves towards the sofa and carefully positions himself on the edge, allowing his feet to dangle above the floor. As he gradually leans back, he feels the cushions' softness enveloping his body, providing a sense of relaxation and comfort. He takes a deep breath, feeling the warmth and cosiness of the room surrounding him.

He watches Jade finishing to cook.

"Do you think the police will do something to your ex?"

"I don't care. I hope they catch him...He deserves it."

Jade exchanged a look with Simone.

After putting the food on the plates, Jade starts bringing the dishes to the table.

"Can we not talk about him? I swear I feel shit just thinking about his name."

"Okay. I'll let it go."

"What is your opinion of the old woman? Do you believe that everything that is happening is predetermined by fate?"

"You did something nice for her, and she returned the favour."

"Also, this morning, I didn't even have my coffee for the first time, and this happened. Think about it...Sometimes, it's like a wake-up call...I think in life, we should slow down and savour every moment. What do you think?" Says Simone.

"I agree with you."

Jade carefully sets the plate of food on the table and steps towards Simone, her eyes intently on him. As she approaches, she can feel her heart rate increase. She reaches out to Simone with her hand, resting it gently on Simone's arm.

Jade interrupted the conversation and asked if she could say something. Simone responded in a very gentle way:

"Sure, babe. Tell me."

Jade then took a deep breath and looked intensely into Simone's eyes as she declared her love for him. The air was filled with a mix of nervousness and excitement as both of them felt the weight of the moment. Simone's heart skipped a beat as she realised the depth of Jade's feelings.

"I love you," Jade says

"I know you do…"

"No, no… Listen for a second."

Jade looks deeper into Simone's eyes this time.

"I love you…"

"Our love remains unwritten, a tale waiting to be told, filled with the most exquisite moments of passion, boundless joy, and unwavering devotion. Our love is a force that transcends the boundaries of time and space, destined to last for eternity. It is a radiant flame that illuminates our way through the darkest of nights and a gentle breeze that caresses our souls with its tender touch. In this world of chaos and uncertainty, we have found solace in the loving embrace of each other, and our hearts beat as one in perfect harmony. With every passing moment, our love grows stronger, deeper, *and more intense as we journey together towards a future filled with infinite possibilities and endless happiness."*

25

AMSTERDAM - SEPTEMBER 2023

With a focused and unwavering look, Jade fixates on the handsome guy walking outside, delving deep into his soul with a piercing gaze.

As the guy feels someone's eyes on him, he turns around with his headphones dangling around his neck, exuding a charm that's hard to resist.

The two individuals lock eyes in a silent exchange, holding their gaze fixed on each other for several tense seconds.

The guy accidentally collided with someone with his bicycle because he was distracted by looking at Jade.

Feeling slightly flustered, the guy offers a sheepish smile in response to the collision. Jade can't help but grin as she watches the humorous scene of the guy carelessly colliding with someone while walking on his bicycle.

Jade is still sitting there, gazing at the tranquil scenery before her. The trees sway gently in the breeze as she's lost in the guy's smile.

Out of nowhere, the guy's gaze became fixated on the scene unfolding within the confines of the cafe. His attention was drawn in, and his focus intensified as he took in the details of what was happening.

Jade turns around as a man approaches her seat.

As Tiberius reaches out to touch Jade's hair, he notices how it cascades down her back like a waterfall of ebony silk. The strands are so fine and delicate that he can't help but marvel at how they feel between his fingers. He steps closer, inhaling her sweet scent and feeling her warmth against his skin. With utmost care, he gathers a few strands of her hair and twists them around his finger, savouring the texture and the way it bounces back into place. And then, as he leans in, he gently kisses her cheek, relishing the softness of her skin and how she responds to his touch. It's a moment of pure tenderness and intimacy between them that he knows he'll cherish forever.

She turned again towards the outside to see the shock on the handsome guy's face and wondered what he would think now.

Jade watched intently as the handsome guy, whose face had suddenly fallen, pedalled away on his bicycle. His posture was slumped, and his movements appeared sluggish, as if he was carrying an enormous weight on his shoulders. She could almost sense the sadness emanating from him. As he gradually receded into the distance, Jade's eyes followed him until he was nothing more than a speck on the horizon. It was as if a part of her wanted to call out to him, but she knew it would be futile. She turned back to Tiberius with a heavy heart and smiled at him.

Jade sits next to Tiberius, lost in thoughts, wondering who the handsome stranger is and what happened. The encounter leaves her with unease as if something important was left unsaid.

As she contemplates the possibilities, she realises that she may never know the answers to her burning questions. The mysterious man had left an indelible mark on her mind, and she couldn't help but wonder what could have been if they had met under different circumstances.

The end...